ARLENE COTTERELL
AND PHILIP OLONZO HITE

WHERE DOES DESTINY LEAD TO?

Where Does Destiny Lead to?
Copyright © 2023 by Arlene Cotterell and Philip Olonzo Hite

ISBN
978-1-959365-99-0 (Paperback)
978-1-961117-00-6 (eBook)
978-1-959365-98-3 (Hardcover)

TABLE OF CONTENTS

CHAPTER ONE

THE NIGHTS WERE ALWAYS TREACHEROUS and tonight commenced the same, only to worsen. Somewhere from high above, there came crimson glazed skies hand-in-hand with loneliness escorted by a blind fury which was accompanied with a wretched awareness that Beelzebub was near to pilfer a soul, any wretched soul predestined to the depths of hell. Somewhere from high above in the crimson glazed skies the moon became surrounded by iridescent angels gallantly dancing about the moon, their souls eager to entertain love's languishing defeat. It had been said that if you tune your mind as the angels chanted, your next breath would be subdued making it incipient to all the rest. What does destiny lead to ? It is true boys and girls things do go bump in the night but things also go bump in the day.

My name is Philip and I am a medical assistant at the hospital. Good day to you. I would like to know if the parents have ever wondered where all those children that vanished during the day as well as in the night that have never been found were actually at, so they could be found and sent home to be reunited with their families. Who, or as Philip might have declared, what abducted their children for there were many other children that were not abducted.If the children left behind had marks, they were just a pigmentation thing that people knew to be birthmarks.

The children that were abducted had a specific mark in an not so obvious place for the minions to pilfer only them from the surface of the earth and get taken to the depths of hell by desperate fallen angels that were in service to Beelzebub, having no choice but to reside in hell for all eternity. That was when Philip knew for a fact that the fallen angels had taken the children which brought back all the details to him from when he was trapped in hell it was not easy for Philip to re-live, for it brought back awful memories of the torture. Demons were to pilfer only specific children from the surface of the earth to get taken to the depths of hell by desperate fallen angels that were in service to Beelzebub, having no choice but to reside in hell for all eternity.

That was where Philip knew for a fact that the fallen angels had taken the children from these colonists. What became of those children you dare to ask? Well, being one-hundred percent accurate with the details was not easy, for it brought back awful torturous memories. Philip was forced to face his mind into helping children who were in hell right now. Philip needed to focus on the task at hand and give the community the answers they were seeking. The children that were abducted had a specific mark for the demons to pilfer only them from the surface of the earth and get taken to the depths of hell by desperate fallen angels that were in service to Beelzebub, having no choice but to reside in hell forever.

Well, being one-hundred percent accurate with the details was not easy, for it brought back awful torturous memories Philip was forced to face his mind into helping children who were in hell right now. Philip needed to focus on the task at hand and give the community the answers they were seeking. The children that were abducted had a specific mark for the demons to pilfer only them from the surface of the earth and get taken to the depths of hell by desperate fallen angels that were in service to Beelzebub, having no choice but to reside in hell for all eternity. That was where Philip knew for a fact that the fallen angels had taken the children from these colonists. What became of those children you dare to ask? Well, being one-hundred percent accurate with the details was not easy, for it brought back awful torturous memories Philip was forced to face his mind into helping children who were in hell right now.

Philip needed to focus on the task at hand and give the community the answers they were seeking Philip had to move in steps one at a time in order to satisfy the crowd. Philip warned all the families that those answers would prove gruesome and difficult to accept, especially if they were the parent of one or more of those children because the first thing to know was that the demons did not plan on ever letting those children return to their homes.

The children were in hell for an eternity unless like Philip they could find a way to successfully escape. That was a nearly impossible thing to do especially since Philip escaped and all the minions were ordered to search the complete areas of hell for any more possibilities of clean escapes.

Philip knew he had to help those children but knew he could not save them alone. Philip suddenly remembered that Jesus had told him to call upon him if he needed him at any time. Right as Philip was about to summon Jesus the parents interrupted Philip and his train of thought demanding to know how Philip knew so much about the current topic. It appeared he would have to delve into his own past through present in reference to his personal life which he was extremely leery of . Philip had hoped to keep his events with the fallen angels as well as with the heavenly angels to himself.

The new information about his experiences would change things and provide the parents that were gathered around to expect much more from him than what he could provide alone. From being able to escape without being caught the demons had rewarded Philip with the gift of not bothering him anymore. That could change if he were to return to hell, nothing was mentioned about a situation of any kind about any run-ins. Philip was forced to face his mental aspect of his experience into helping the children who were in hell right now.

Philip needed to focus on the task at hand and give the community the answers they were seeking. The children that were abducted had a specific mark for the demons to pilfer only them from the surface of the earth and get taken to the depths of hell by desperate fallen angels that were in service to Beelzebub, having no choice but to reside in hell for all eternity. That was where Philip knew for a fact that the fallen angels had taken the children from these colonists.

What became of those children you dare to ask? Well, being one-hundred percent accurate with the details was not easy, for it brought back awful torturous memories Philip was forced to face his mind that was running like a picture show over and over into helping those sickly, scared, and close to death children who were in hell right now, Beelzebub would never see the infiltration coming which would make the recovery of the children an advantage for them. Philip needed to focus on the task at hand and give the community the answers they were seeking

Philip had to move in steps one at a time in order to satisfy the crowd. Philip warned all the families that those answers would prove gruesome and difficult to accept, especially if they were the parent of one or more of those children because the first thing to know was that the demons did not plan on ever letting those children return to their homes. The children were in hell for an eternity unless like Philip they could find a way to successfully escape. That was a nearly impossible thing to do especially since Philip escaped and all the minions were ordered to search the complete areas of hell.

Making the others do what they did not want to do was not the right thing to do because this was a society of free will, all Philip could do was to pray for them and continue to show them the right way to handle things. The huge problem was that Philip was not dealing with normal people, he was dealing with frantic parents of children lost in the depths of hell. Those parents were convinced at the thought that Philip could possibly go to where the children were and bring them back to the surface, into the loving arms of their parents, who would take them home. Philip understood that these parents would go through great lengths to get their babies back, without thoughts of what the steps to getting their babies back would place Philip into.

Ultimate danger could possibly place him in the position to be trapped in the depths of hell alongside the children. He was there to bring out and save those children with the help of the divine ones which would ultimately place those children back into the loving arms of their families and friends. This is where Philip realized the gates of hell were opening for hopefully just one last time and that was for Arlene to be taken under to hell by minions to be Beelzebub's wife and mother to all of the children he had abducted and finally to create together the ultimate child who would hold the powers of every living thing below and above.

Jesus interrupted Arlene's descent which was why she was taken sickly not only had Arlene been chosen to be the mate for Beelzebub since her birth by his choice she had also been chosen by God since birth to be special and do immaculate things for God through Jesus and become angelic with wings but had not grown them yet. She would have the ability to go into the heavens where all of God's angels and Jesus would go. It would be a joyous time for all and a great feeling of succession for Philip for he always wanted to do something great and selfless in his life that would change something in society whatever big or small and it appeared that his opportunity was upon him but which road would be the route to getting Arlene closest to her destiny? Beelzebub never had a clue that he was going to lose the children and Arlene nor did he know that he would be imprisoned for the rest of eternity; it was obvious what Beelzebub and his minions' destiny was.

Philip was still on his knees, but he was praying more seriously and directly now more than ever that Jesus would guide him on which path to take. There were only two options: retrieve the children from hell which was risky or walk away from the whole situation and never look back. Philip's mind was consumed with fear but his gut feeling, and his heart were optioning for saving those children and confronting the possibility of things going poorly. Philip felt that the lord was giving him a direct go ahead to save those children and that he would be with Jesus the entire time and would keep everyone that needed to get out safe and sound, so Philip stood up and called for the attention of all who gathered around expecting to get their precious loved one back. As all the expectant parents as well as the other family members and friends gathered around and grew silent Philip prepared his words carefully so he would not add to the anxieties of the people and end up in a situation worse than he could imagine.

Now that all were quiet and giving all their attention to him, he began to announce that he received an answer to his prayer and was told to go forth and save the children and Jesus would be with them and they would all be delivered from any harm whatsoever, is that where destiny started to lead to for those children? Now it was time for Philip to go underground to retrieve the children but first he had one more thing to say and he addressed the people and advised them that they needed a warm blanket for each child coming out from the depths of hell because they would be coming from temperatures over one hundred degrees up to the surface where it is only seventy degrees.

It would be quite cold to them so on that note the mothers started to scramble towards their homes to acquire a blanket so they could urgently return to where they could welcome their children home as soon as they came up from the depths of the earth's many layers. Now the final moment that everyone was waiting for, Philip to jump into action then suddenly the earth started to quake then a hole opened in the ground exposing hell for Arlene to descend and take her place to rule underground at Beelzebub's side, as his equal where Philip was standing. He finally submerged into the massively thick earth down to the depths of hell seemingly without hesitation. However, the lack of hesitation showed Philip showing full faith as without it he would not be going back to the place he luckily escaped from and had feared recoil from all his life.

AsPhilip fell through the many layers of the earth, he could feel the body of Christ intertwining with his. It was so intense that there was no way to mistake what Philip was feeling; it gave a sensation as being produced by God himself. Philip felt a rather majestic feeling but no second went by where Philip took that feeling upon himself to where he took credit for the stimulating intertwining of the two bodies, he simply gave glory to God. Philip moved on to do what he was there to do and in his continuous fall never put forth any thought as to what the next step was to be, he just figured he would deal with things as they came and respond to those things as Christ prompted him to do. That would be the only way to get himself and all of those children out of the belly of hell without harm.

Philip wrapped in the protection of Jesus' hands finally landed at their destination and were noticed by Beelzebub instantly then within seconds the minions realized that Philip and Jesus were there so the minions gathered the children and surrounded the children in a circular pattern to try to keep them from the hands of Philip and Jesus. Neither were afraid of Beelzebub or his minions. Jesus and Philip simply approached Beelzebub and Jesus ordered Beelzebub to call back his helpers and for everyone on the dark side to stand down because with or without force the children would be going above and getting reunited with those who cared for them, primarily their parents, and the same went for Philip.

Beelzebub and his crew knew they were no match for Jesus, but they would not give up without a fight because that was just their nature even though they already knew they would lose. Jesus started to reason with Beelzebub in explaining that they had children of God and that God had not forgotten about them. It just was not time to get them back yet but now it was time and so it would be. The current mission was a mission of God the father not Jesus or Philip they were just pawns in completing the mission at hand.

Jesus went on to mention that Beelzebub had been neglecting the children by keeping them malnourished, they got what little fluids they sweat off their brow that flowed down to their lips and licked off then for their substance they got from the bodies of souls that Beelzebub took prematurely the children were emaciated and weak at that rate it would be very soon that they too would perish, Philip and Jesus were there to take them home and nurse them back to health and help them to rise above the mental anguish that the whole experience had put them through which Philip and Jesus assumed would take some time and it would depend on the strength of each child's mental status if they would come out of the experience or not, if so how well.

What they did not know was that the children would talk amongst themselves when Beelzebub was not within hearing distance to keep their morale alive and help one another stay sane. Jesus proclaimed that he was going to start acting after warning Beelzebub of one thing and that was that God had already had plans of punishment for Beelzebub and his minions once the children and Philip were safe and sound then it would be time for Jesus to act, and he did. Belzebub and his minions would be meeting their absolute and final destiny for God was ready to take their wicked ways and deposit them into a vault that there was no escaping from.

First there was to be a face to face standoff so Jesus approached Beelzebub with no space left between them then Jesus whispered let my children go followed by Beelzebub hissing as he replied to Jesus a simple no. Jesus turned from Beelzebub and turned towards the minions then shot fire from his fingertips at the minions and they hysterically jumped back deforming their circle around the children then Philip called for the children to hurriedly come to him, and they rapidly did as Philip had asked them to do. In the meantime Jesus was still dealing with Beelzebub which was continuing to allow Philip to get the children to safety. At the hole where Jesus and Philip had come down to hell, suddenly there were the same amount of God's angels as the amount of children, fifty-five.

The angels advised Philip that they were sent by God to take the children to the surface and it would be quicker with them helping than with just him doing it so Philip thanked them graciously and felt that the lord was giving him a direct go ahead to save those children. Philip had to trust that Jesus would be with him and everyone the entire time keeping everyone that needed to get out safe and sound. Philip stood up and called for the attention of all who gathered around expecting to get their precious loved one back. As all the expectant parents as well as the other family members and friends gathered around and grew silent Philip prepared his words carefully so he would not add to the anxieties of the people and end up in a situation worse than he could imagine. Now that all were quiet and giving all their attention to him, he began to announce that he received an answer to his prayer and was told to go forth and save the children and Jesus would be with them and they would all be delivered from any harm whatsoever, is that where destiny started to lead to for those children?

Now it was time for Philip to go underground to retrieve the children but first he had one more thing to say and he addressed the people and advised them that they needed a warm blanket for each child coming out from the depths of hell. The children would be coming from temperatures over one hundred degrees up to the surface where it was only seventy degrees, it would be quite cold to them so on that note the mothers started to scramble towards their homes to acquire a blanket. They went speedily so they could urgently return to where they could welcome their children home as soon as they came up from the depths of the earth's many layers. Now the final moment that everyone was waiting for, Philip to jump into action then suddenly the earth started to quake then a hole opened in the ground exposing hell for Arlene to descend and take her place to rule underground at Beelzebub's side as his equal where Philip was standing. Philip finally submerged into the massively thick earth down to the depths of hell seemingly without hesitation. However, the lack of hesitation showed Philip showing full faith as without it he would not be going back to the place he luckily escaped from and had feared recoil from all his life. As Philfell through the many layers of the earth, he could feel the body of Christ intertwining with his and it was so intense that there was no way to mistake what Philip was feeling; it gave a sensation as being produced by God himself.

The continuous fall never put forth any thought as to what the next step was to be Philip just figured he would deal with things as they came and respond to those things as the Christ prompted him to do so that would be the only way to get himself and all of those children out of the belly of hell without harm. Philip, wrapped in the protection of Jesus' hands, finally landed at their destination and was noticed by Beelzebub instantly. Within seconds the minions realized that Philip and Jesus were there so the minions gathered the children and surrounded the children in a circular pattern to try to keep them from the hands of Philip and Jesus. Neither were afraid of Beelzebub or his minions and they simply approached Beelzebub and ordered him to call back his helpers and for everyone on the dark side to stand down because with or without force the children would be going above and get reunited with those who cared for them primarily their parents, and the same went for Philip.

Beelzebub and his crew knew they were no match for Jesus, but they would not give up without a fight. That was just their nature even though they already knew they would lose. Jesus started to reason with Beelzebub in explaining that they had children of God and that God had not forgotten about them. It just was not time to get them back yet but now it was time and so it would be. The current mission was a mission of God the father not Jesus or Philip they were just pawns in completing the mission at hand. Philip was overjoyed to be helping God through Jesus. Then Jesus went on to mention that Beelzebub had been neglecting the children by keeping them malnourished. The children got what little fluids they sweat off their brow that flowed down to their lips and licked off, then for their substance they got from the bodies of souls that Beelzebub took prematurely, the children were emaciated and weak at that rate it would be very soon that they too would perish. Philip and Jesus were there to take them home and nurse them back to health and help them to rise above the mental anguish that the whole experience had put them through.

Philip and Jesus assumed it would take some time and it would depend on the strength of each child's mental status if they would come out of the experience or not, if so how well. What they did not know was that the children would talk amongst themselves when Beelzebub was not within hearing distance to keep their morale alive and help one another stay sane. Jesus proclaimed that he was going to start acting after warning Beelzebub of one thing and that was that God had already had plans of punishment for Beelzebub and his minions once the children and Philip were safe and sound then it would be time for Jesus to act, and he did. That was where Belzebub and his minions would be meeting their destiny for God was ready to take their wicked ways and deposit them into a vault that there was no escaping from. First there was to be a face to face standoff so Jesus approached Beelzebub with no space left between them then Jesus whispered let my children go then Beelzebub hissed as he replied to Jesus a simple no. Jesus turned from Beelzebub and turned towards the minions then shot fire from his fingertips at the minions. They hysterically jumped back, deforming their circle around the children, then Philip called for the children to hurriedly come to him, and they rapidly did as Philip had asked them to do.

In the meantime Jesus was still dealing with Beelzebub which was continuing to allow Philip to get the children to safety. At the hole where Jesus and Philip had come down to hell suddenly there were the same amount of God's angels as the amount of children, fifty-five. They advised Philip that they were sent by God to take the children to the surface and it would be quicker with them helping than with just him doing it so Philip thanked them and turned the children over to the angels of heaven. Philip then went half way back to where Jesus was to keep the minions away from the angels and children should they get the idea to go try to interfere with the removal of the children, even though the angels were speedy about getting a child and going above ground. Finally, the angels and children were gone and that just left Philip and Jesus so Philip went over to Jesus. Jesus started to reason with Beelzebub by explaining that they had children of God and that God had not forgotten about them. It just was not time to get them back yet but now it was time and so it would be. The current mission was a mission of God the father not Jesus or Philip they were just pawns in completing the mission at hand.

Jesus went on to mention that Beelzebub had been neglecting the children by keeping them malnourished, they got what little fluids they sweat off their brow that flowed down to their lips and licked off then for their substance they got from the bodies of souls that Beelzebub took prematurely. The children were emaciated and weak at that rate it would be very soon that they too would perish, Philip and Jesus were there to take them home and nurse them back to health and help them to rise above the mental anguish that the whole experience had put them through. Philip and Jesus assumed it would take some time to recover and it would depend on the strength of each child's mental status if they would come out of the experience, or not, if so how well. What they did not know was that the children would talk amongst themselves when Beelzebub was not within hearing distance to keep their morale alive and help one another stay sane. Jesus proclaimed that he was going to start acting after issuing warnings.

Jesus reasoned with Beelzebub in explaining that they had children of God and that God had not forgotten about them. It just was not time to get them back yet but now it was time and so it would be. The current mission was a mission of God the father not Jesus or Philip they were just pawns in completing the mission at hand. Then Jesus went on to mention that Beelzebub had been neglecting the children by keeping them malnourished, they got what little fluids they sweat off their brow that flowed down to their lips and licked off then for their substance they got from the bodies of souls that Beelzebub took prematurely the children were emaciated and weak at that rate it would be very soon that they too would perish. Philip and Jesus were there to take them home and nurse them back to health and help them to rise above the mental anguish that the whole experience had put them through which Philip and Jesus assumed would take some time and it would depend on the strength of each child's mental status if they would come out of the experience or not, if so how well.

What they did not know was that the children would talk amongst themselves when Beelzebub was not within hearing distance to keep their morale alive and help one another stay sane. Jesus proclaimed that he was going to start acting after warning Beelzebub of one thing and that was that God had already had plans of punishment for Beelzebub and his minions once the children and Philip were safe and sound then it would be time for Jesus to act, and he did, that was where Belzebub and his minions would be meeting their destiny for God was ready to take their wicked ways and deposit them into a vault that there was no escaping from.

First there was to be a face to face standoff so Jesus approached Beelzebub with no space left between them not even a piece of paper could slide between them. Jesus whispered to Beelzebub let my children go then Beelzebub hissed loudly as he replied softly to Jesus a simple no. Jesus turned from Beelzebub and turned towards the minions then shot fire from his fingertips at the minions and they hysterically jumped back deforming their circle around the children. Philip called for the children to hurriedly come to him, and they rapidly did as Philip had asked them to do. In the meantime Jesus was still dealing with Beelzebub which was continuing to allow Philip to get the children to safety. At the hole where Jesus and Philip had come down to hell, suddenly there were the same amount of God's angels as the amount of children. The angels advised Philip that they were sent by God to take the children to the surface, it would be quicker with them helping than with just him doing it. Philip then gave the children to the angels and thanked them wholeheartedly. Philip then went half way back to where Jesus was to keep the minions away from the angels and children should they get the idea to go try to interfere with the removal of the children. Even though the heavenly angels were speedy about getting a child and going above ground, cautions still needed to be implicated.

CHAPTER TWO

JESUS PROCLAIMED THAT HE WAS going to start acting after warning Beelzebub of one thing and that was that God had already had plans of punishment for Beelzebub and his minions once the children and Philip were safe and sound then it would be time for Jesus to act, and he did, that was where Belzebub and his minions would be meeting their destiny for God was ready to take their wicked was and deposit them into a vault that there was no escaping from. First there was to be a face to face standoff so Jesus approached Beelzebub with no space left between them not even a piece of paper could fit between them. Jesus whispered let my children go then Beelzebub forcefully hissed as he quietly replied to Jesus a simple no. Jesus turned from Beelzebub turning towards the minions then shot fire from his fingertips at the minions. The minions hysterically jumped back, deforming their circle around the children, then Philip called for the children to hurriedly come to him, and they rapidly did as Philip had asked them to do.

In the meantime Jesus was still dealing with Beelzebub which was continuing to allow Philip to get the children to safety. At the hole where Jesus and Philip had come down to hell suddenly there were the same amount of God's angels as the amount of children they advised Philip that they were sent by God to take the children to the surface and it would be quicker with them helping than with just him doing it, Philip thanked them and turned the children over to them then went half way back to where Jesus was. Philip wanted to keep the minions away from the angels and children should they get the idea to go try to interfere with the removal of the children, even though the angels were speedy about getting a child and going above ground. Finally, the angels and children were gone and that just left Philip and Jesus .

Philip went over to Jesus to help where he could, but Jesus advised Philip to go on ahead and he would see Philip on the surface, so Philip did as he was told. When Philip was close to the hole, he began to make out a figure at the hole it looked like God had sent an angel down for him also. Once Philip was taken to the surface by the angel and saw all the children, he noticed that all the angels who assisted with the escape plan were going back down the hole where Jesus still was. Philip guessed that they were going to help Jesus eliminate Beelzebub and his minions. However, one of the minions escaped without anyone else noticing. The minion faded into the community gathering as much information as possible along the way to somewhere to blend in or hide, the minion found a great nearby host to live inside of, that host was Arlene. No one was guarding her and was busy with other things and would not notice the change in her. Jesus was standing toe to toe with the evil lord of darkness and the angels formed a half circle behind Jesus to help conquer the minions and there was a heavy sense of God's hand protecting Jesus and his angels. Finally, Jesus took in a deep breath then with all his might he blew his breath at Beelzebub who then froze over like an ice sculpture then the angels of God did the same to the minions of Beelzebub and they too froze over. then all of a sudden the hands of God swept the minions and their ruler of the dark up into his mighty hands and took them all up into the heavens then the angels and Jesus hurriedly went to the hole and headed for the earth's underground surface as hell began to crumble around them and would never open back again.

Finally, Jesus and the angels made it above ground and Jesus made his way to Philip then thanked him for his service. Jesus plucked one of his largest feathers from his wings and gave it to Philip telling Philip that it was a special gift that was a precious gift of gratitude and would assist him in summoning Jesus when he was needed. Philip was to hold the feather in his hands and call on Jesus by name and Jesus would appear as summoned. Philip moved on with more things to discuss one thing was how he was overwhelmed with all the new changes and he told Jesus he was nervous about being ruler of the people Jesus let Philip know that his job was ongoing with his people then Jesus hugged Philip and informed Philip that he was the people's ruler and when it was time, he would have to choose who would take his place as ruler of the people when he needed to step down. Philip acknowledged Jesus and replied that he would always consult with Jesus and follow what the father and son would advise him to do. Jesus finally went to the heavens then Philip turned his attention to the people and noticed that the children were still in the area where the hole used to be and even though they were covered with blankets they were shivering something terrible, so it was time for Philip to do his job and take action to focus on the children and start their care. Philip's shaky legs carried his body over to the children and their mothers. Philip would advise the mothers to take their children into their homes and clean them up then feed them bland food that would be easy to consume and be sure to give them fluids that would be hydrating and finally letting the mothers know that he wanted to meet with all the mothers, fathers, and saved children at a certain time that would allow more than enough time for the mothers to care for their children because it would be most urgent to get started with the mental aspect of the help for the children.

Helping the children would help the parents in helping to care and support their children. The parents could call on Philip at any time who in turn could call on Jesus and the angels. The angels had not left yet and would stay with their appointed child until God said otherwise. In the meantime, God was dealing with Beelzebub and his crew. Just because they were frozen and got broken into many pieces did not mean they were relinquished at all; they were very much alive and still able to create commotion. God had brought them to the heavens where there was a door that led to a place that resembled purgatory and was for dark angels and their followers and once locked away in that place, they would never see the light of day again nor could they cause any commotion. Now back to the children even though they were in bad shape they were still physically fixable and mentally reachable that could not be where their destiny led to. As for the children's angels they did as Philip's angel Jesus had done, they plucked a special feather from their wings and gave it to their appointed child and told their child that it was special and they could use it to summon the angel at any time and they would come to them for they were not just appointed they were their guardian angels for all of their lives and they felt blessed to be there for them.

All the children suddenly remembered how to smile when they received their feather so the angels returned to the heavens so the mothers could bathe the children and get them into clean clothes while the fathers were preparing a meal for their family to sit together and enjoy a meal together once again. After their meal, they would gather for a meeting that Philip would like to hold; it was essentially mandatory. The family members could not fathom what the purpose of the meeting could be for but Philip was using the meeting time to start to bring the children back into their society and work through the mental anguish so they could live happily like the abduction encounter never happened. The meeting was to reach out to the children and try to get their attention by getting them to acknowledge their names and possibly engage in some sort of communication. Philip was also going to have all the hospital doctors there to assess the children for any medical assistance that may be necessary. Right now, the children were eating with their family members and doing a fantastic job of eating and consuming liquids. They were already getting some of their color back into their faces and they were requesting second and third helpings of food, that was an excellent sign.

The parents did not speak to their children at home because of the situation they just came out of. The parents were not sure how to approach their children, so the parents were following the children's interactive progress. After getting some nutrition there was to be a meeting at the religious hall, no one knew exactly what the topic was but they did know it was important to bring their children. Now at the religious hall the parents found a place for themselves and their children to sit. Now with the whole town there, it was time for the ones who called for the meeting to take place to start the meeting. The meeting was called to be by the hospital's doctors so they could get the children admitted into the hospital at no cost to the parents. One of the young female children went upon the podium and listened carefully to what the doctors were conversing about. Apparently the doctors were concerned about the parents giving consent for their children to be hospitalized for an unknown period of time. The parents would be able to visit their babies at visiting hours, and the best thing about the situation was that the whole thing was at no cost to the parents. The child listening to all that grabbed the microphone then began to speak into it and tell the rest of the children as well as their parents about what she had heard. When the doctors realized what that female child was saying word for word they rushed over to her to take the microphone from her but once there they stopped by her as the parents listened to her and started to ask questions. That was when it was time for the doctors to take the microphone and address their public. The children also listened carefully and understood everything.

One by one the children started getting up and joining the two girls up front until finally all the children were up there, now it seemed that this situation could open the doorway to their destiny. The parents questioned their children on why they were up there, Philip used the microphone again and explained to the parents that their children were voluntarily willing to be hospitalized to get better the right way so they could truly live happily with their families and not be sick all the time. The parents understood and all at once the parents started to thank the doctors and verbally cheered their children on. It became clear to Philip that there was nothing to do with the mental status of the children they were tough and whatever Beelzebub did to the children they did not allow it to break them, they even stood not just as individuals, those children were incredible their parents were learning of this also and they were proud of their children it was as if the situation never happened. Business regarding the children had been addressed. It was now time to leave the meeting place which was the religious hall to make the necessary accommodations. The parent's needed to get some items for their children to take to the hospital. That would take about an hour. One of the doctors went to the microphone and directed the parents to bring their children to the hospital in about an hour. In the meantime the parents needed to take their children home to get some comfort items and a few things to help pass some time comfortably while being in the hospital for the children. The doctor finished by letting the people know that the hospital was opening two wings and setting things up where the children would be all together. The families all called out their Thank Yous as they were leaving to take their children home. They needed to gather some items in preparation for their possible elongated hospital stay. One of the girls was reading a four-book series before she was abducted and only got half way through but remembered how amazing the story line was so she wanted to take the series to the hospital to have Philip read out loud and share it with all of the children and just start over for her they were a memorable series and one you cannot resist reading over and over, there were twenty-three boys there and thirty-two girls for a total of fifty-five families that had been affected by the abductions. The series books were just as good for boys as they were for girls the author of the books was a new author named Arlene Cotterell the first book was Legend of the dinosaur tail then Life in the legendary city of gold then Danger in the land of grandeur and finally, The transformation of life to legend.

The environment those children would be released from the hospital was a very small city surrounded by a giant country setting with so many different animals that were not disturbed by the presence of humans. In fact there were some families that lived in the country areas and had made friends with the wild animals. By the time the children would be able to leave the hospital, the world they would be going out into would have a strange resemblance to the world that the book had for their people. It would be eerily easy for the children to adjust to because of hearing the books being read to them during the reading session from Philip. On the way to the hospital Jesus accommodated Philip to discuss the taking down of the city buildings, while converting the space into forest landscape to allow the total island to be as it was before they got there. That would allow the animals to live among the humans. Jesus also let Philip know that his time would be focused on the children while he and his fellow angels would take care of the restoration of the island and Philip felt that Jesus' idea was a grand one and Philip even told him so then questioned if God the father would be lending his personal touch also then Jesus simply replied yes. Philip agreed that the plans for the new forest area and lack of a city was a necessary yet grand idea and mentioned that if there was anything he could do to help just to call upon him. Jesus agreed and expressed his love verbally then turned to fly back to the city area where work had already begun by the angels.

The only building that would not be taken down but would be added on and be made more up to date and beyond would be the hospital. As Jesus was going back to the city building God insisted that they leave the hospital as it was and add an outer crust to it that would make the hospital look like it was made out of wood not metal and cement Jesus complied and pulled the angels together telling them what the father had strongly recommended so the angels acknowledged and went directly back to work to fulfilling God's order. Finally, Philip arrived at the hospital to spend some time with the children as he had promised and when he walked into the area where the children were and they were able to see him they all called out his name as to invite him in and he called out to the children that he was there for them then they grew silent. The girl with the book series called Philip over to her bed so she could make him aware that she had the book series and that she wanted his assistance in sharing them with the rest of her friends. Philip took the books as she was handing them to him. The girl gave Philip intricate descriptions of all four books and felt that the books were something special and figured he too would become a part of the books as well. He happily told the girl that he would love to assist her in sharing the books with everyone and that he was anxious to read the books for himself. He could let her know that he would read daily if the rest of the children wanted him to share it with them. He would address the group with the same talent that she had used then after a few seconds he changed his mind and decided to have the girl address the children the same way she had done to him so when he had mentioned it to the girl she was very willing and moved to the foot of her bed and sat up onto her knees. Philip gained the focus of the children then the girl spoke to the group the same way she had done to Philip and the children all excitedly agreed to have some reading time because when the girl gave the pitch, the children became inquisitive as to where the books led to they all wanted to start their reading time that day. Philip suddenly got two ideas. The first was to get a microphone with several speakers that the microphone could wirelessly sink with for all of the children to be able to hear him read the books. Secondly was to surprise the children all with their own sets of books and a set for himself then he could return the set of books he had to the girl that rightfully owned them. Instead of reading the first books on that day Philip briefly informed the children of his two ideas and they encouraged him to handle his ideas first.

He could use his ideas on the day when it would be ready then Philip thanked the children for their approval and understanding and immediately turned to exit the hospital to put his ideas into effect. Philip's first stop was to visit the little shop that would make copies of the books so he ordered fifty-six copies of each book in the series so each child and he would have a copy of each book in the series and he would return later to pick up the fifty-six copies in the meantime Philip would be at the mini shop looking for a few wireless speakers that would automatically sink with a specialized microphone. He found just what he needed right away so he found the shopkeeper to discuss the price and information on how to use the items properly. The salesman explained everything and once Philip was satisfied with the information he let the shop owner know that he was ready to purchase the items so they went to the checkout stand and performed the sales transaction. There was a hefty load of books so the shop keeper had one of his employees load his horse driven wagons with the books. He would also help Philip give the sets of books to each child until all books were given out and each child had a copy. Philip was appreciative of the help that was sent with him and when he tried to offer a tip for the service, the helper refused compensation. stating that it was the very thing that Jesus would have done by order of the father the thanks you could show was for him and all of the children to read the books in sequence and entirety, then show the author how you felt about the finished series and to be honest. The shop keeper then told Philip that there would be no charge for the books since the production of the books was a divine order to be done right away and under those circumstances, he would be stealing money from the people, that would be like stealing from the people and from God that was a punishment waiting to happen to Philip and the shopkeeper.

Philip went back to the hospital with the children having the speakers and microphone in tow to set those things up and while getting those items uploaded Philip was speaking to the children and telling them that he had a special gift for them, once it was finished at the shop where it had to be made a buggy would pull up at the main entrance. A buggy driver and Philip could start to bring the gifts in. The gifts were for everyone so everyone was getting one. This was just so the children knew it was ordered by God the Father for Jesus to be the head of the progress of the gift to be done accurately and quickly. Suddenly the main doors of the hospital flew open and there stood the man from the book shop. He had a satchel over his shoulder packed full of packages. The shopkeeper stepped in a little so Philip, knowing who the man was, got closer to the man and took the satchel then set the satchel aside giving the man a hug and kiss on the cheek. Philip then took the shopkeeper inside of the hospital to grab a giant hospital cart and the two men went back out to the buggy and filled the cart with the rest of the book packages. They wheeled the loaded cart into where the children were. Philip and Jesus noticed that the man and his buggy were nowhere in sight so Jesus and Philip were left without an extra set of hands to give each child a package.

The girl that owned the book set that the other children were getting was being given a special and rare one of a kind bookmark that was owned by a special individual, the author of the series named Arlene Cotterell. It was being handed down from the special and rare collection of personal bookmarks. Every child was asked not to open their package until told to do so they waited as told to do but each one of the children were anxious to find out what they got. When everyone got a gift Philip told all the children that they could open their package but treat it nicely and to be careful opening the surprise, so the children did as they were told. Philip and Jesus knew when the children got their packages open because there were suddenly verbal noises of gratitude and verbal sounds of pleasures and the girl that already had the books, she got a special book mark from the author of her series of books she was sobbing tears of gratitude and asking if she could visit the author as soon as she was released from the hospital. what no one knew was that the author had already left her home that was in the neighboring city and on her way to the hospital to see the girl who got her book marker and to purchase several sets of books for herself to have a set for herself and some to hand out to a few people that live in her colony and signed by the author soon it would become known that author Arlene was working on another book and how far it was going to go was up to God and Jesus. This writer did not write herself; she wrote what gracefully came to her no matter what time of day or night.

The new book could be one book or more and how many more was up to divine contribution. Anyway, Philip stayed with the children while Jesus went on to see if the author was willing to bet that the girl did not have a book marker which ended up being true. Philip tapped the girl on the shoulder and when he did the girl looked up. When she spotted the woman next to him her eyes grew large then she looked at the back of her books and realized that the lady was not just any lady it was Arlene the author of her book set. The girl jumped to her knees on her bed and threw her arms around Arlene's neck as she began to tell her how wonderful the books were and how neat the author was for what she had learned about her. Arlene asked the girl if she liked the bookmark and the girl picked it up and began to talk very fast about how the bookmark was special to her and how she needed something like that previously she had been using a scrap piece of paper, but the special bookmark was just perfect for a gift and no other gift would compare.

Arlene took the first book of the series and wrote all the ways for the girl to contact her as well as signing the book with a personal message then when she was done she handed the book back to the girl then asked how she could get in touch of the girl because of her dedication to the authors books she was willing to send a copy of her books as they came out to the girl complimentary, meaning at no cost, it would be another gift so the girl got a piece of paper and wrote her information on it. Arlene took the paper as she told the girl it would mean a lot if the girl would give her some feedback on the books she sends her so she could use her feedback to continuously write better and better, the girl promised she would do that then Arlene thanked her and went to the next child in line. Arlene continued to make her rounds until she met and conversated with all of the children and Philip again. Although Arlene and Philip felt great about Arlene being able to take the trip to visit the children, something did not feel right, Arlene made that known to Philip so he suggested that they go to the cafeteria and get something to eat and maybe it would help.

That sounded like a good idea to Arlene since it had been some time since she had last eaten. Philip and Arlene noticed the angels had gotten with the city structures and were making the hospital look like a wooden made building instead of making a new building and finalizing it with everything inside being functional the hospital had to stay open at all times and that was why it was decided that it was best to give the hospital an outer look of a wooden structure. The outer structure of the hospital was complete, and the city area was close to being done, all the angels had to do was fill the new void with forest flooring and plant some shrubs, small as well as big . That was where the father spoke to his son Jesus and Jesus spoke to the people there advising that they all needed to leave the area and go home for at least an hour then the city area would be completely transformed and ready to be occupied by all. The angels were to go back to the heavens as well as Jesus. While in heaven and cleaned up from the dirty chore Jesus had just engaged in, he approached God the father and asked if they had completed what they were supposed to do The father replied that they did more than what was expected so Jesus questioned if there was anything more, they could help with then the father replied in due time.

All the children were finally settled down and laid back in their beds and reading their books while they made various noises as they read, Philip even had the same reaction as he read. The nurses and doctors as well as other hospital staff that walked by heard the children as they passed by and concluded that they too needed to have the series of that line of books. The main hospital doors started to open and who else than the author of the book series walked in and headed to the nurse's desk and inquired for the whereabouts of a man named Philip and many children that would have come in all together and the nurse informed the author that she could escort her to the crew she was asking about. The nurse walked from behind her desk to guide the author to the children and Philip and within five minutes the nurse got Arlene to the children and Philip. Arlene glanced at the children and Philip then turned to speak to the nurse but she had walked away to get back to her post and the author just stood at the doorway and watched the children read and listened to their verbal reactions they were so involved in their books that they had no clue what was going on around them so Arlene walked on in and tapped Philip on the shoulder with one hand while motioning with the other hand to be silent so when Philip looked up he saw her motion and he complied.

Philip and Arlene walked outside the room to talk and that was where she introduced herself to Philip and he to her. After introductions and some exchanges of a personal yet professional level the two of them decided to go back into the large room and introduce the author to the children starting with the girl that originally had the books and received the book mark from the author since everyone was getting books which she already had so the next thing she would need was a bookmark. The two of them finally headed to the cafeteria. Just past the nurses desk then going down the hall towards the cafeteria Arlene fell to the floor and was turning blue and violently shaking about. Philip did not know what to do because somehow something about what happened did not seem to be a seizure, Philip ran to the nurse's desk and requested that she call for a doctor to immediately get to where Arlene was and call now then he turned and went back to Arlene. On his return Philip noticed that Arlene was essentially blue all over and barely breathing but she was no longer shaking. Finally, a doctor was running up the hall to find out what the dire emergency was and when he reached where Philip and Arlene were he carefully listened to Philip as he was assessing Arlene.

The doctor went into action immediately and used Philip as his assistant and first thing was first her airway so the doctor ordered Philip to care for her airway by handing him resuscitation equipment. Fortunately, Philip knew what to do with all the parts to put it together then he also knew how to use it correctly. In the meantime nurses were establishing an intravenous access and the porter went for a gurney so they could transfer Arlene from the hallway floor to a personal room with a bed and admissions would then work on admitting her while the doctor worked on finding out what kind of ailment was occurring in Arlene's body so they could fight it and get her all better. Philip abruptly realized that he had seen that very thing that happened to Arlene somewhere before and many times. Philip was straining his mind to try to remember where he was when he had seen this very ailment, then it all came back to him. It was while he was in hell the minions would inhabit the bodies of newcomers and because the human body was not strong enough to maintain the minion they would cause the human body to do as Arlene's did. In a few days the human was dead and the minion was stronger and the cycle would repeat. Philip quickly found the doctor who was working on Arlene and pulled him aside to explain what he had discovered. At first the doctor did not believe what Philip was rambling about until Philip grabbed the doctor by his upper arms and gently shook him saying that he had been through the same thing and he could help bring Arlene back to them.

The trick was to capture and destroy the minion then things made sense and the doctor thanked Philip and agreed that Philip was to be in charge of the feat. Philip would coach the doctor every step of the way. Philip notified the doctor that the process of catching the minion would take more strength and specialized talent in dealing with things of that nature. Philip informed the doctor that he must go home for a spell to get his feather that he left behind from Jesus to summon him. He would get Jesus there at Arlene's bedside and start the process and the doctor agreed to stay at Arlene's bedside to patiently wait for them to get back. Philip left immediately for home to get his summoning feather that Jesus had given to him. Along the way Philip was thinking that if one minion had escaped as the hole in the ground was closing, how many more minions if any was able to escape hell to live above with the people and carry bad intentions and with that thought Philip had planned to give that question to Jesus.

Philip finally got home and went straight to his bedroom to get his feather. With his feather Philip knelt on his knees and summoned Jesus for an important feat that could not wait. Jesus appeared before Philip then he questioned him about what could be so life threatening that his summons held a desperate feel to it. Philip replied that the situation was life threatening due to the fact that a minion had escaped hell and was now residing inside of Arlene. He needed Jesus' help to get it out of her while catching it and relinquishing it, that would be the only way to save her life. Philip asked Jesus if he would know if there were any other minions that could have escaped just like the one in Arlene. Jesus replied that yes he could fix Arlene and take care of her minion, he could also find out if there were any other minions on the earth that may have escaped. Jesus told Philip to take his hand and with one breath they would be at Arlene's bedside. Philip did as Jesus said to do and sure enough, they were right at Arlene's bedside the doctor did as he said he would do, that was to stay there awaiting the return of Philip with Jesus in tow. Jesus raised both arms into the air and summoned his angels to bring the demon lock box and do so hastily. Within a few seconds two angels appeared with a small golden box with a lock. The two angels held the box at Arlene's mouth then Jesus spoke to God the father and without haste Arlene started to cough and gag then some fluid started to emerge, it went into the lock box the fluid took about twenty minutes to get into the lock box before Arlene quit coughing and gagging. Jesus announced that the minion was now in the lock box in its entirety. The angels took the lock box into the heavens to be put into the portal of demons to never be heard or seen anymore. Jesus stayed behind to bring Arlene back from the brink of death and after that she would have to stay in the hospital for a few days to sufficiently recover before returning to her normal activities.

Philip and the doctor hugged Jesus and thanked him for the miracle he had just performed. Then Philip questioned Jesus as to whether or not any more minions had been roaming on the earth. Then Jesus reported to Philip that he had all of God's angels searching and taking count of all minions to make it boldly clear what was where, and they should be done in just a few minutes. In the meantime, the doctor was continuing Arlene's care as directed by Jesus. Finally, the census was finished, it was official that the minion that was in Arlene was the only one that had escaped hell to reside on earth. Jesus had caught him so now everyone would be safe from that issue. Now that Arlene was alert and found herself in the hospital, she wanted to know exactly why she was there and when she could leave. Jesus moved his body up to her field of vision right away so everyone could remain calm. The doctor explained that a minion had escaped hell and took residence in her body which was slowly killing her; they had to summon Jesus to exhume the minion. Now it was time to nurse her body back to the healthy state it was in prior to the invasion. Then Arlene stated that she had to stay in the hospital longer than Jesus replied for a few days or so, just until her body was able to support itself on its own. Arlene settled down and agreed to stay for however long the doctor said she would need to be there.

Jesus ascended to the heavens. Philip left to go back to the children while the doctor continued to care for Arlene. As soon as Philip entered the giant room of the children, they told Philip that they were aware of Arlene being in the hospital and they wanted to go see her to lift her spirits, then requested that Philip escort them right away. With understanding Philip informed the children that it was against the hospital rules to do that. Philip was willing to stick his neck out this time because it would be just the thing Arlene needed so all the children got out of their beds and formed a single line. They followed Philip to Arlene's room and somehow nobody saw them, which was fabulous. Arlene just happened to look up from hanging her head down and low and behold she saw children filling up her room, that gave her a warm feeling in her heart. She told the children to gather closer to her bed and she let them know that they were just what she needed and that she loved each one of them. Philip had an idea that simply popped into his mind so he left in search of the doctor. When Philip found the doctor he questioned the doctor if it was possible to move Arlene into the room that the children were in. The doctor replied that it was a superb idea and would be therapeutic for all involved

The doctor asked Philip if he was willing to help, Philip replied that he would do whatever was necessary to get them together. they went to Arlene's room and told the children to go to their own beds right away so they did then the doctor let Philip know that it would take at least the two of them to move Arlene's bed into the children's room then Philip replied to just do it and together they each took a side of her bed and started to roll the bed out of the room into the hallway towards the children's room. The two men now had Arlene's bed at the doorway of the children's room and this was where it would be quite some work, they had to really maneuver the children's beds but both men were stubborn and did not like to leave anything left undone so they gave the beds their best and got Arlene's bed in its cove and got Arlene settled in then the children started to cheer and thank the two men for making the suggestion come to life. Now both the children and Arlene were all satisfied, and everyone was headed for a complete healing and a long relationship.

In all of the communications carried out between Arlene and the children it came up that all but one of the children got a wrapped gift of their own and it was the book series written by Arlene the one girl that did not get a set of books was given a bookmarker that was very exquisite given to her from the authors personal collection since she already had the full collection of books. The next task was to make a clear book cover so it would keep the actual book covers last longer and Arlene could show them how to do it. It was a simple craft to do and the hospital had everything they would need to make the book covers. The children could even design their book covers if they wanted to. Arlene did not think the children would not want to decorate their book covers since that would cover up the book's original design. It was important for the cover design to be seen.

Suddenly, all fifty-five children went unconscious and stopped breathing and Arlene knew she could only help by hitting the emergency buttons on the walls, so she got out of her bed and went to each bed pushing each emergency button then she got back into her bed. Within seconds a whole slew of nurses rushed in and proceeded to put all the bed heads down and legs down then the nurses hollered to get some doctors in there. They started cardiopulmonary resuscitation. Arlene realized that if there were going to be any doctors in the room she would have to summon them so Arlene unhooked herself from her monitors, oxygen, intravenous access without taking the IV out just unhooking it from the main line , and anything else that needed to be unhooked from. Finally, she went to the nurses desk and found a nurse at the desk and explained that the children were all undergoing cardiopulmonary resuscitation. The nurses needed some doctors in there so the nurse at the desk got on the speaker system and called to all available doctors being needed in the deluxe children's room immediately. Before Arlene could start to walk to her room there had to be at least ten doctors running from wherever they were to where the children were. Arlene stayed at the nurse's desk for about eight minutes so as not to get in the way of the doctors, and give some time for late responders.

While Arlene was waiting at the desk the nurse offered to reconnect Arlene to her monitors and get her all situated and comfy, Arlene thanked the nurse so together, they followed the last doctor into the children's room. Part way into the short walk to the children's room where Arlene's bed was she started to tell the nurse that was with her that she suddenly felt weak, light headed and had sharp shooting pain in her chest that radiated into her jaw down to her arm. Right then they were at Arlene's bed so the nurse helped Arlene into her bed and started to quickly hook Arlene up to all her gadgets, the most important things first and it appeared that Arlene was having a heart attack. They needed a doctor over with them so the nurse called out for a doctor and one came rushing over right away. A doctor assed Arlene then informed the nurse to lay the bed flat and to get the setup for intubation, they would take things from there as they came. Fifty-five children were being bagged. The other doctors requested for the children to be intubated for now and they would try to be extubated as soon as possible. All the doctors ordered a lot of blood tests and several other tests that were not done by blood to try to diagnose what was going on.

What commonality did the fifty-five children have and possibly what Arlene may have had, if any. The doctors felt that it was time to call in the parents to discuss what their children were doing up to the time they were taken, then their medical history. The doctors would then talk to Philip about what the children may have been going through while with Beelzebub and what type of condition they appeared to be in when brought back above. The doctors saw the case as a puzzle that needed to be put together and they were great at puzzles. It would give them the answers they needed to help the children and possibly Arlene to recover from such an abnormal set of symptoms that were worsening as the minutes went by. Finally, the parents started to trickle in so the doctor could get each of the girl's and boy's health histories right after that Philip walked into the room to check out the children when the doctor plunged on him wanting to know what the children went through while being underground, Philip began to tell everything to the doctor. The doctor knew it was extremely difficult to discuss the matter as Philip began to weep softly while moving along and finishing up with the true story of what it was like living in hell. The doctor gave Philip his condolences while thanking him for helping with knowing their latest medical history which would certainly help with the children's treatments. Philip and the doctor straightened themselves up then went on to talking to the parents of the children and writing everything the parents had to say.

The doctors were finished with the parents and they advised the parents to go home and get some rest so the parents did just that with one demand and that was for the doctors to keep the parents updated on how their children were doing good or bad and the doctors let the parents know that they would have the charge nurse call them with the updates so the parents thanked the doctors for the deal and worked their way to the main exit to go home. Once outside Philip scrambled to get outside before any of the parents could get too far away so he could get them together and set a time for them to meet with him at his home for the better of their children and the parents were okay with that. A time was set for them to meet as soon as Philip got off work and fulfilled his travel time from the hospital to his arrival home then they would immediately start their meeting to hopefully complete the meeting in time enough to allow for the parents to return to their homes at a decent hour in the evening.

Basically, the meeting was to update the parents on the condition of their children and explain why the things that were happening and offer a basic game plan of how it would be addressed. Philip informed the parents that when the doctors met all together, they would include him and he understood everything that basically the children were doing well with such as low level of care, and not so good things such as their bodies starting to reject what treatment was being offered which was low level of oxygen supplement as well as high amounts of fluids and steady amounts of nutrition. Now their body temperatures have dropped and their bodies were no longer being supported by their bodies as before so all of the children were under warming blankets and intubated since their bodies were no longer wanting to support their respiratory system and they would be inserting another tube for feeding so the children could continue to get adequate nutrition and of course the children would be observed closely and any further action needed would be addressed as it came, they were considered critical and would be treated aggressively. However, all the doctors were sure they could treat the children with a full recovery in the end and once that was achieved, they could be sent home without any further sickness from that sort of ailment ever again.

Now for Arlene, she needed a sort of different care with some minor similarities. She was carefully examined by several of the doctors and found that she was not having a heart attack and her respiratory drive was well intact and functioning at peak performance so she would not need to be intubated at that time, that meant that the doctors could extubate her. However, her temperature was rising, and they had to put a cooling blanket over her opposite of the children and the doctors had two large bore intravenous accesses established and were giving her cold fluids to help her cool down, Arlene was still somewhat conscious. Philip was able to explain to the doctors what was going on with Arlene, she was still alert enough to verbally back up what Philip was speaking of plus offer some more information that Philip did not know of the serious intricate details that were supposed to stay between her and Beelzebub. Those intricate details were what the doctors needed to know in order to save her life for what the doctors knew prior to the deep secrets would not have helped in her care. Arlene began to explain to Philip and the doctors that she remembered Beelzebub visiting her as an infant up to the present.

He spoke to her and slowly groomed her to be his wife and the mother of all the children in hell. She was also groomed to bear him, the ultimate child who would hold all the powers that exist on earth and in heaven. He had actually made some changes to her body over the years to help her withstand the environment of hell. Now that all of that had been completed, she has gone into shock because she is not in the environment her body believed it should be in. Now the most important task at hand and possibly the only one that could save her life was to change the things that Beelzebub had changed and put her body back to how it was naturally supposed to be. That would most likely need a miracle from God himself because the doctors in the hospital did not have the means or know how to tamper with genetics in that way. Philip also informed the parents of the children that while he would be praying to God for Arlene that he would also pray for each individual child as they were not getting any better either. The parents were grateful for Philip's updates and for being direct and not holding anything back. They made sure to express their gratitude to Philip then the meeting was finished as Philip informed the parents that he would call another meeting when he had enough information to share, the parents all thanked Philip as they sobbed God bless you and walked out of his home to go to their homes.

Everyone was at home and seated at their diner table getting ready to say grace when all of a sudden, their angels appeared and proclaimed to have a message for them from God himself and the other families were also getting the same message from their guardian angels that on the morrow bright and early go to the hospital and stay for two hours for God the father will be doing some work on the land for there will be no more city it will soon be all country and God the father will also be working on each and every home and the people will roam about with the wildlife as one and they too will befriend you all you are all to become a people of one. The angels ended their words with the good news that God the father would flow through each child and Arlene right before they arrived at the hospital. They would be in for a wonderful surprise as well as the doctors but they must control themselves and allow the doctors to do their work. They had been working throughout the night, everyone agreed and gave thanks, then the angels left so everyone could finish eating their dinner and prepare for bed to get some extra sleep. They knew they would need the extra sleep because according to their angels the upcoming day would be a very full day. They must be on their toes to expect anything, especially things out of the ordinary that only God could do either himself or through Jesus, not even the angels could handle such a feat.

Even though Philip was home and should have been sleeping in preparation for an upcoming busy day, he was on his knees praying to God for Arlene to be pulled out of harm's way that Beelzebub had placed her in. Philip prayed for each child by name that they would be restored to their normal healthy selves and keep healthy as they continue to grow. Philip made sure to ask God for the children to be able to recover enough to make a good life for themselves. By the time Philip finished praying there was still a small fraction of time that he could get in a cat nap prior to going into work. He knew after his day was to wind down, he would get to bed very early to try to make up for the sleep he had lost if that was even possible. Throughout the night while everyone in the community slept Jesus was at the hospital tending to Arlene and each child individually so when the doctors made their next rounds on them, they would find them all awake and wanting the tubes removed along with the heavy warming blankets over them. Arlene managed to kick off her cooling blanket and right as Jesus finished and vanished into thin air A doctor appeared in the room that Arlene and the children were in and found them all awake and very active. The doctor fled to the nurse's desk and ordered her to get on the horn and get as many nurses as possible into the children's room immediately because there was about to be a party.

The nurse at the desk did just what the doctor asked. She picked up the speaker phone and ordered that all available nurses report to the children's bay immediately. The order came straight from a doctor's mouth. Within several minutes after the request of needing nurses in the children's bay, there were nurses and doctors coming from every direction possible. The doctors responded simply because there was a call for so many nurses and usually when they had a call for nurses like that there was something very wrong and life threatening, so they just wanted to be there just in case they would be needed. The nurses and doctors flooded the children's bay and noticed that the children were alert and seemingly ready for extubation. The doctors verified that by calling out that each doctor needed two nurses, one on each side of the bed, that they were going to extubate the children and Arlene. Everyone was in their required place to care for the children and Arlene. The first thing at hand was the doctors finally got everyone needing tubes extubated and were now without tubes. It was obvious to the charge nurse at the front desk for she could faintly hear all the raspy forced chatter coming from the children's bay. The very next thing to do was to take off the soft restraints that were placed around the children's wrists to keep them from pulling their tubes out of their lungs which was a natural response.

Philip was witnessing the miraculous changes that the children and Arlene seemed to have undergone and was very excited and thankful. Philip broke out in prayer to thank Jesus and God the father for their help in the matter and finished with telling Jesus that he remembered to not leave the hospital until the two hours was up and informed Jesus that he would remind those at the hospital of that. Philip closed his prayer and entered the children's bay to make rounds and visit with each child and Arlene one by one. It was a fascinating experience and very fulfilling to know that everyone one of the affected patients had such a profound recovery that was done by God himself, what a special gift. All the patients even commented that they felt the hands of God taking away the things that Beelzebub had imprinted onto them. Now their spirits felt so light and free, they stated that they were ready to leave the hospital and go out to the community to work for God and show their gratitude for what God and Jesus had done for them and of course their angels. The doctors said that they needed to stay a couple more days for observation to ensure nothing else needed to be dealt with, if nothing else aroused then they could go home and do whatever it was that they had to do within their parents guidelines and of course God's guidelines as well. Arlene and all of the children agreed to the next few days in the hospital since they knew they had many more days to be on earth. They wanted to spend their lives out of the hospital with Arlene in their lives . The children had gotten attached to her and wanted to have her in their lives for the rest of their days, they were also waiting to see all the next books Arlene would write and publish.

Arlene lived in the next town over and the people there did not know her as an author; to them she was just another towns member so she would not be missed. With that in mind Arlene informed the children that she would have to go to the next town over upon release from the hospital and collect her belongings. After purchasing a home in their town and making the big move into their town so she could be near the children, all of the children cheered and offered their fathers and their wagons and horses so she could move in one trip. When their families would visit them that day they could let them know what was about to transpire and beg them for their help. Arlene explained to the children that what they proposed was very caring and definitely honorable, but their parents did not deserve to be forced to help. A simple question of offering their help with a chance of replying no would be the preferred way of conducting the situation. The children thought about the offer Arlene put before them and agreed that her way was most logical and all at once bolstered out vocally that her suggestion was best and they would use her idea. It was about visiting time so Arlene and the children settled down and prepared the best they could for their visitors and sure enough the visitors arrived on time.

After greetings the children delved into serious conversation about the male visitors helping Arlene move her belongings from the next village to their village and without hesitation the fathers replied of course and the mothers butted in and offered to make a great variety of a feast that would suffice for lunch and dinner with the accompany of desserts and beverages. Arlene had no visitors as she was not married and had no children or family members for when God built the new earth, her family was not saved. You see she was not the only person who had no family but her family along with other families damned themselves by denying the word of God. In the eyes of the children and their families Arlene was a part of their families and she would never be lonely. All of the parents formed a line to speak to Arlene so they could inform Arlene that she was a part of their family and they would take her in as one of their children. She was not to be shy of asking to fulfill any needs or desires and finally that even though she had a home of her own she was welcome to their homes at any time. The parents' offer was so sentimental that she had no wants and she knew she would not grieve for her original family anymore. After all the parents had their time with Arlene, visiting time was over so everybody had a chance to say their goodbyes and go back to their day.

Once the visitors left Arlene quickly started to speak and she addressed the children positively for sharing their families with her. She was very appreciative of them and now she was excited to make her move from the village where she currently resided to the children's village. The children and Arlene stated that they did not have to order their fathers to help with the transition they just simply needed to ask if they were willing to help and told them of the situation and now the children could be with Arlene anytime, it was just a matter of waiting to be released from the hospital. The days went by fast and before anyone knew it, it was check out time from the hospital. All of the girls and boy's parents were outside waiting for their children and there was another couple whose child had grown and moved out on her own and they were waiting for Arlene. The couple was there to help Arlene just as the children had their parents, since their child was grown and moved out to live independently. Arlene thanked the couple for taking her on as an adopted child and willing to keep her under their wings for as long as possible. Soon the couple would be taking her on a small trip to meet their real daughter so she would be an honest to goodness child of theirs. They knew that their real daughter would love her as they did. Now every set of parents had left to go home to set their homes up for their children and get them settled in. This was an overdone process and everyone was over excited.

The couple that was there for Arlene took her to the community stables. Once there the couple got Arlene some horses hooked up to a wagon they bought for her then got her upon her wagon to follow them to their home. Once there they would get Arlene settled into their home until she could get ready to travel to her home, load up and return. The sire of the small humble family would follow her and help Arlene to help make the journey easier. Their child by blood had just arrived at their home with the mother and got things ready there. When the sire of the family and Arlene would be ready to travel, the community would build a house for Arlene. A house on the neighboring property that their child did not want and that would be as close as possible to the parents and child that were there for Arlene for the rest of their days on the new earth. The new home for Arlene would also be in the circle of the route for the rest of the children so all of the children could be close to her. When the rest of the children found out the living situation for Arlene, they too wanted their fathers to help. Instead of demanding their fathers to help the children's cause they simply asked if their fathers would kindly assist in the move. Of course the rest of the families were on board to assist in any way they could. Arlene gave a date and leave time and that was when the crew left with all the assistance it only took one time to go out and one time back.

All of Arlene's belongings were at the new home site. That was when the mothers and daughters started to decorate and clean the home. The boys did the outside of the home to make it pretty and cleaned up with some outdoor furniture and enough for having some company as well as being welcoming to the animals, so they could come up close and eat out of the dishes provided for them. There were dishes hung for the flying animals and dishes in appropriate areas for the land animals both on the ground and a bit higher for those who were a bit taller. The older couple took Arlene to their home to have meals at the times that meals came around and Arlene would be with the couple until her home was ready, there would be no peeking at her home. To get an idea of what Arlene liked the older woman took Arlene window shopping in the shopping square as they discussed the many items she liked in each shop and the older woman was paying close attention so she could gather up all the women who were working on Arlene's home to tell them her findings. As fun as it was to window shop and dream of having certain items in their homes, it was also time to head back to the older couple's home to prepare the next meal so they could stay nourished and get a break from all the work they had been doing.

During the meal the three of them would discuss all the nice items Arlene admired in the shops, while the old woman wrote down the items in her lap in detail, along with the names of the shops they were in. The old man kept the conversation going to keep the attention off of the old woman so as to not let Arlene notice what the old woman was doing. Right after cleaning up from the meal the old woman would tuck Arlene into bed for a midday nap. With Arlene napping, all of the women in the village could meet in the food hall to share the list of desires that Arlene had unsuspiciously made. To assist the women in putting some things up for trade to get some things for Arlene's home, the old woman would wake Arlene and occupy her while the rest of the women would go out together and see if they could get as many of the items on the list as possible, if not all of the items. As the women got ready to leave for the food hall their husbands stopped their wives and informed them to take their list of things to barter with and all the women took their lists and found from a quick glance that the husbands had all added things to the list and the women hugged their husbands in tears and thanked them. The husbands told their wives' that Arlene would do the same and she was already family. Now with every woman darting for the chow hall and the men rustling out to their jobs Arlene was fast asleep.

It was time to get some work done and soon because the old woman had to be back home before Arlene awoke. Now all the women were dashing to the marketplaces so they could purchase all the things on their list and get it back to the cottage they were fixing up for Arlene. Hopefully they could have it completed that evening. As for the older lady who had taken in Arlene, she got home just in time for Arlene to awaken it seemed because when she entered her home Arlene was looking rested and moving all about so the older lady timidly walked over to Arlene and rubbed her head gently which assisted in waking her peacefully. Arlene thanked the woman for suggesting the nap and for helping her awake easily and the woman told Arlene that it was no bother it was a mommy move she had learned when her daughter was young and the technique still worked on her grown up baby to that day. Arlene asked the older woman who she was because she put herself after Arlene and others so when Arlene questioned her, she replied that the lord had touched her heart and told her to take her home and be a mother to the grown child. Arlene repeated that she was touched to be a mother for her and the woman replied yes. It was already a blessing then Arlene replied that she agreed that it was already a blessing then the older woman told Arlene that her first name was Sheayle and that since she was now her new mother she could just call her mama. Arlene told mama that she would really like that. Suddenly with a second thought Arlene asked mama if that meant that her husband was now her papa and mama replied yes, Arlene was overjoyed.

What Arlene did not know and was not to know was that mama was taking her under her wing because there was a lot of issues for Arlene to work through mentally and physically with the changes that Beelzebub had made to her since birth to prepare her to be his bride and the mother of the children that he had in hades The most minor issue was that Arlene was not aware of any of that. Some of the changes were going to be nearly impossible to get over and others will seem easy but some of the changes only Arlene would notice, mama would have to trust that Arlene would confide in her. You see mama was not just some human who was willing to follow the promptings of Jesus, she was an angel that God had sent to live on earth to fit in with humans in preparation for the work that led ahead with Arlene, the work that Arlene was to go through could kill her. God knew ahead of time that it would take the talent of an angel to help the Arlene child through the changes she would have to go through. On a lighter note, one of the ladies that was working on the home for Arlene had dropped by mama's home to let her know without letting

Arlene know anything that her home was complete. Everyone was ready for whenever it was thought appropriate to walk Arlene over to her new home. Mama acknowledged and thanked the woman then said they would walk her over after dinner and to spread the word amongst the other women and their husbands who helped make everything come together financially. The only time mama saw Arlene's home was when everyone went inside to find out what they had to work with, if it was going to be easy or hard, and it fell in the middle so mama could not wait to see the home now. Mama felt that it would not feel the same and that her newfound daughter would love her new home.

Now papa was walking through the front door, and he was hungry, so mama got dinner on the table as quickly as possible while Arlene helped Papa sit down as mama got the little things done and did not have to worry about having Arlene in the way. Finely, the meal was ready, and mama sat down at the table and papa said grace then everyone began to eat and to mama's surprise everyone was famished, before long dinner was over, so papa went to the living room to relax while the two women cleaned up the dining room and kitchen. As soon as everything was done there was a knock at the front door, so papa answered the door, and it was a lot of couples wanting mama and papa to bring Arlene and for them to come along and go out for a short time and that mama already knew of the arrangement, so papa called on mama to come to the door and she did then she called out for Arlene, and she summoned papa and explained that someone had a surprise coming to them and the community was going to come together to give one large surprise gift. The next thing to tackle was the barn behind the house so Arlene could use it for her horses and other animals she may get from the community.

This unveiling was important and no one could fathom what the author's reaction would be. The people would be in for a surprise to see Arlene's reaction. Mama explained to Arlene that the community pulled together and had put together a super surprise for someone in the community. It was time to present the gift, so everyone had to be there where it was and as a new member of the community she had to be there also. Arlene was good for it but then mama blind folded her and took her by the hand saying that she was the guest of honor. She did not need to see the gift until everyone was ready and it was time, which meant that everyone was gathered around where they could see the author. That was important because they set up a room just for her to work on her books in. Now they were all at the new home for Arlene and all were ready, so mama took Arlene inside and removed the blind fold. Mama told Arlene welcome home this is your new home. The community ladies got together with their husbands and rebuilt the house and the ladies finished by making sure the inside was decorated and had the necessary items in it. With the whole community working together they got it done rather quickly. Mama informed Arlene that the immediate outside was cleaned up so she could enjoy the outdoors for a spell but that there was a barn out back and the men were going to get together and fix it up so she could use it for her horses and buggy and any other animals she may get in the near future. Arlene stood on her porch and faced the crowd saying that she loved how beautiful and practical her new home was. Arlene expressed how surprised she was that the people already gathered all her belongings from her other home she was moving out of, and had it all in her new home. Arlene thanked the community women for how fashioned they decorated her new home.

CHAPTER THREE

ARLENE HUGGED MAMA AND GAVE her a personal thank you then told mama that they would be speaking about the new home later and mama just smiled softly. Finely, all the people started to trickle off and return to their own homes, so it was now an enjoyable time for mama papa and Arlene to all go back to mama's home and have the conversation that Arlene mentioned having later while in her home. Before Arlene could speak her mind mama quickly started to talk about how beautiful Arlene's new home was and she even brought up the fact that one of her rooms was devoted to her writing and that the window provided a great view then mama advised Arlene that the sooner she moved into her new home the quicker she could settle in and get to writing and schedule her time with the children and other things she needed to do. Now With high society clothing and so fourth she could comfortably mix and mingle and maybe catch the eye of a gentleman caller. Even the kitchen supplies were fully stocked with a large variety of things to cook with. Some things easily prepared for those late nights when cooking just was not going to happen. When Arlene had noticed that she suspected that the women had the entire house done the same way, fully loaded for what each room was representing, she just had to go check immediately to find out if her suspicion was correct. To Arlene's surprise all was well stocked for every big and small item.

Finally, Arlene sat in one of the grand chairs in the living room and all of a sudden Philip jumped right into Arlene's mind then all Arlene could think of was him. After a short while Arlene sprung to her feet and decided to go to the hospital to see if she could find Philip. Now Arlene found herself at the charge nurses desk. Arlene questioned the charge nurse about Philip's whereabouts. The nurse informed Arlene that Philip was in the doctor's lounge getting ready to go home. Arlene ran to the doctor's lounge to wait for him to walk out, then she grabbed him by the hand and asked if she could walk him home because she needed to discuss something with him. Finely, he came out of the doctor's lounge and as was planned Arlene grabbed Phillip by his hand and pulled him out of the pack of doctors that were more than ready to go home to get some sleep then to spend some time with their families before going back to the hospital. Now that Arlene had Philip pulled aside she revealed why she separated him from the pack then Philip replied that he was beside himself and that it was more of an honor that Arlene held him on a pedestal. Arlene mentioned that she had feelings for him and she was blunt in asking him if he would give her a chance to make him a happy husband. He now had the opportunity to reply that he had feelings for her also and he was trying to find a way to get some private time with her.

Since the time off was a four day stretch of time, Philip asked Arlene if he could go home and get cleaned up, pack a few things, then be sotraight on his way to Arlene's. Arlene let Philip know that was just fine and she would be waiting for him so when it was time to get comfortable on Arlene's part she would sit on the couch. When Philip arrived he put his luggage in her bedroom then returned to be at her side. They started talking about simple things which turned into personal things, which revealed how alike they were, which led to them falling into love at first sight, which kept growing as the hours and days went on. Now after several weeks passing by the love between them led them to the warm welcome of discussing marriage. Both of them were feeling the same about that thought. They both felt that it was time to move on into husband and wife territory. They discussed the wedding to figure out where to hold the wedding so all the villager's could attend. The two of them decided to have the wedding at the church hall then the reception at the chow hall where the food would be available to all, there would be some games and other things for the children to have fun playing with. Arlene made some invitations and got them out to the people and made it clear that the festivities would be in two days from the current day. For the next two days Philip made the transition from his home to Arlene's home and with her help they got everything in its place and it still looked loving and felt soothing.

Now the day had come and it was only four hours until the wedding so the mythological members gathered around Arlene and got her into her wedding attire then they did her hair up with flowers and then Philip was pulled away from Arlene so the rest of the mythological members were with Philip getting him to looking handsome and finding a small group of flowers that would match Arlene's bouquet just a fraction of her size of flowers to put on his suit jacket. Everything was finished right on time for the beginning of the time that was allotted for the wedding to take place and everyone was there and seated and the bride and groom were where they were supposed to be and now the wedding began. The male pegasus carried Philip while the female pegasus carried Arlene and that made the look that everyone was shooting for. In the crowd of everyone viewing the wedding several individuals were crying in sentiment and beauty of the service. The wedding was coming to a close so those who were sobbing dried their tears and pulled themselves together. Now it was time to go to the chow hall where the reception was to be held along with the things that were added for the children.

Suddenly the lord appeared and called for the attention of all there. Once all were quiet and offering their complete attention to Jesus, he spoke to all that were there which was the entire community. Jesus announced that now Philip and Arlene have been joined as one they by default would be the king and queen of that particular city, all cheered for a brief moment. The people returned to a state of humbleness so Jesus could finish what he went to the city to tell the people what was necessary to tell them. The last thing to tell the people, primarily the new king and queen, was that although the city now had a leader they still had to find a couple to stand by and step up when the time came. They needed to learn everything possible so once it was time for the current leaders to step down they would already have things set up with no delay to make the transition quick and comfortable. Once the Lord was completely finished with the necessary business at hand he stayed for a short time and spoke to the newlyweds about doing just what God had wanted them to do. Philip and Arlene were extremely thankful to have pleased God and had hoped to continue to do so. It was time to clean up and bring the small community back to normal then all could get back to their day whatever was left then close shop and go home to enjoy spending time with their families.

Once everything was cleaned up the children that were in the hospital with Arlene gathered around her and excitedly spoke to her about her other books saying they were on the next book and it was very enticing. Now all was done and the children's parents were calling for them but before moving about their way the children made a time and day to get together. They wanted to read and frolic; they could even have a picnic. All agreed that would be nice and everyone decided that they all would make it happen then the children gave Arlene hugs and kisses on the cheek then ran off to unite with their parents. Arlene and Philip went home to spend the rest of their wedding day together without any interruptions. One thing led to another and the two of them were led to consummating their union. After they laid on the bed together caressing one another and talking about how they wanted their future to turn out. All of a sudden Arlene felt a sharp traveling pain for just a few seconds then it went away. Arlene and Philip believed it was due to the fact that the sexual encounter was her first experience in that area as well as his. He was wondering if he could have done something wrong and hurt her somehow. Philip had not discussed what he had already thought about in his mind and that was if Arlene had another pain of any kind that involved her reproduction areas and/or any bleeding no matter how light or heavy. He was going to get her to the community hospital to get checked out because the pain was not normal and a slight flash of blood on the first time was normal but no more, Arlene was not aware of the plan because he did not want his new bride to worry he wanted her to have a clear mind to be able to relax with him and he with her.

Now that a few hours had gone by Arlene was still lightly bleeding so Philip requested his wife to get dressed so they could go back to the hospital and get her checked out because she should not be bleeding. Philip admitted that he had planned to send her to the hospital under certain conditions and how she was currently doing fit the protocol. Arlene did not fight his decision on the grounds that he stayed by her side at all times, he agreed so off they went by horseback. Philip kept the horses at a slow walk so Arlene was not jilted, possibly causing her to bleed worse. Finely, at the hospital the two of them dismounted their rides, tied them off and walked into the hospital. Philip asked the charge nurse at the desk right at the inside of the main door if they could check Arlene in. The charge nurse replied that they keep a room ready for them that no one used except the two of them then the charge nurse stood up to go around the desk so she could escort them to their room. From their room the nurse would call the doctor that serviced that room to please come to the room for the queen of the city. The nurse proceeded to help Arlene get changed into a hospital gown then achieved intravenous access in case it would be necessary. Right after the nurse gained the IV access the doctor arrived and introduced himself then asked what the issue was. Arlene looked up to Philip then the doctor blurted out that he did not care who told him the issue but please someone speak. Philip spoke and informed the doctor of what had happened in full detail from beginning to current.

The doctor giggled under his breath and Philip noticed it then Philip questioned the doctor as to what was so funny so the doctor explained that he believed he knew what was going on and it was nothing bad that in fact it was good news but before confirming his suspicion he wanted to do a couple of simple tests that would confirm or deny his suspicion. The first test was a bedside ultrasound. Depending on the results of that test would make it known if they needed to do the other test. The doctor set up the machine which was no work really then he let Arlene know that he was going to put some gel on her low stomache and that it would be cold. It was causing Arlene to jump slightly as the doctor squirted some of the gel on her abdomen. Now was the time of truth the doctor rubbed the gel around with a doppler and finally he was able to see the area he needed to see so he looked very closely and was hoping to find sugestions of life and wham-o the doctor had just found signs of life. He gave Arlene a couple of wash cloths to wipe the remaining gel off her tummy as he told Arlene and Philip that they had just concieved. The doctor informed the couple that the bleeding was nothing to worry about at that time but for her to lay down for some time with her feet up every day until it was time for her to come back for her next visit which would be in two weeks unless there were any reason to return sooner. If he was off duty stay home and send a runner to the hospital to get a hold of him and he would return with the runner making a housecall.

The new couple was informed that if the bleeding got any heavier in the least amount to call out for the doctor and the couple was good for that. The couple was congratuated by the doctor as he was exiting the room. Arlene changed back into her regular outfit then they suddenly realized what the doctor had said. They decided together that they would deal with their reactions once they got home. As the newly married couple got ready to be discharged by the charge nurse the doctor went running up to them and requested to have some blood work done and the couple said no problem. The doctor did the bloodwork and took it to the lab himself but before he left the desk Philip questioned the doctor as to what the bloodwork was for. The doctor replied that he needed to keep track of Arlene's pregnancy hormones just in case she needed to have hormone therapy, the doctor told Philip that he would send for them if they needed to have them come back for the hormone therapy. Meanwhile the children were gathering at Philip and Arlene's home to have their picnic and some reading time. When the new couple got home the children got excited then they asked if everyone was okay and Philip replied that he was just getting home after a visit to the hospital getting Arlene a checkup and that it was found out that she was pregnant and had to be on bed rest with her feet elevated for the next two weeks unless something came up that meant that she needed to be seen sooner.

The children asked Philip if it was okay for them to go inside and have some reading time and lunch they even said please several times. Philip told the children that they could as long as Arlene was feeling well enough then Arlene jumped into the conversation saying that she was fine at the moment but if she started feeling worse then she would let them know and they would have to plan when to get together againe. This day the children and Arlene read into the late evening so when they realized how late it was Philip sugested that he take all the children at once and walk them home. The children were good for that and as usual Arlene thought Philip had a wonderful idea. The children gave Arlene hugs and kisses before leaving. With Philip leading the way they all left and went into a large circle and getting everyone home. Philip speedily went home to watch over his wife who never should be left alone. Right as Philip was stretching out to turn the knob on the front door the doctor moved into Philip's field of vision so Philip questioned the good doctor as to find out what was the purpose of his visit. The doctor replied that he would rather wait until they were with Arlene to share why he was there. When the two men got inside the home they raced to Arlene's bedside then the doctor greeted Arlene while Philip checked on Arlene and coddled her.

The doctor asked the couple for their attention saying that he got the lab results and the results read that her hormones were not high enough in some areas so she would have to get injections regulary and also have blood work with the injections that simple treatment was the full life saving answer to helping Arlene birth a full term living baby. When the couple heard that they were greatful and now more relaxed over the seemingly troubled pregnancy. The doctor was ready to leave as soon as he mentioned to the couple but first he needed to draw some blood and give her the hormone injection and the last thing to inform the couple of was that he was going to do house calls for her instead of hospital visits because of her fragile state. Now the doctor gave Arlene and Philip emotional hugs and reminded them of the day of his return and that it would be on his first day off so he could spend some unlimited time with them and he could offer some respite for Philip to go out to get groceries catch up on chores catch up with the help since all they knew was that Arlene grew ill suddenly and anything else he needed to take care of. Philip did not know but the doctor had some of the community men taking care of the outdoor stuff as well as building the barn and other added on things that would make things easier and finding a young boy to serve them in the barn and cleaning the horses and other care as well as getting their rides ready so they could come and go as desired and the boy would live in a couple of stalls rebuilt to be a bedroom with amneties.

Another thing that the couple did not know that the doctor had planned was to get some of the woemen together and work in cycles so no lady was overworked. Those women were pulling herbs, gathering spices, collecting fruits and vegetables and milking the cows as needed. The women would take turns taking food and deserts to the couple and each woman had to take a turn. It was like taking turns by standing in line and the front person fed the couple until they went to the back of the line and for now it continued until told otherwise by the doctor. Since the new couple had no clue of the doctors plans they did not question his intent with them because that would be considered disrespectfull to your elders and the young ones as well. Now that the doctor was heading back to the hospital he carefully raced the blood samples to the lab and requested the results be brought back stat. As for Philip and Arlene they had noticed a change in their routine but accepted it due to her having to be on bedrest Philip became aware of some of the chores being done on the outside of the home but the couple did not know who to thank for their help. The women that were taking care of the couple inside of the home were just as helpful and worked hard yet fast it seemed that every one knew who did what and they all accentuated one another, it was as if the colony had done this before but they claimed that they had not when asked about the service project as Arlene called it.

The service project, which was what Arlene called it, had been going on for six months and Arlene was doing great. The bleeding had stopped; she only bled for two months. The doctor still wanted Arlene to be on bedrest which was better than chancing anything that could happen there was only three months left. The doctor made his way into the bedroom to check on Arlene while taking some blood work and giving her some hormones according to her last checkup. Arlene tried to put things togerher and came upon the notion that it had to be the doctor that orchestraded the whole thing because it apeared that while the doctor was performing his tasks while the others were working speedingly and everyone finished about the same time. It was not long before the doctor found a young but responsible boy to take care of the animals and if he proved to be the right person for the job he would get a pay raise and keep the barn home then Philip would take him into town and buy him things to personalize his home. After a while once the stable boy was a part of the family the couple would take the stable boy to the center of the community and help him to pick out a horse for his own and every thing that would be needed for him and his horse. The ladies, men, and stable boy were now doing their jobs and the doctor had finally revealed to Philip his plot and that he was trying to keep things from becoming out of control and intimidating.

It came to one more situation which was to tell Arlene or not because neither held secrets from the other then the doctor led his upper body into Philip's upper body and straightly whispered that he should tell his wife that he did not want to be the cause of their possible problems that they had a beautiful relationship with true love and as the justice of the peace said let not another come between them. They were a bit late so both men speedily got to the bedside of Arlene so the doctor could examine Arlene then give her the hormones after taking some blood to test for her hormone levels at that time. At that time the doctor advised the couple that they cold go into labor at any time from the present to being overdue so he gave Arlene a special runner who would stay within sight distance so if she did go into labor the medical runner could get to the doctor who would drop whatever he was doing and head to the doctor as urgently as possible. Once the doctor cleared up some details of what could be upcoming the doctor went to the living room to sit and get himself in order. Philip was informing Arlene of what the doctor had arranged and to what extent. The help was going to continue until the doctor felt that it was safe to drop the level of assistance yet keep dropping the level of assistance until she was post care and recovered from the delivery and used to being a first time mother. then the couple could adjust to getting a new routine which would take some time.

Lastly, the doctor had a freshly retired registered nurse practioner standing right outside the bedroom door out of sight so as the doctor got further in speaking to the couple the nurse was waiting for the cue for her to go into the room with everyone. Finally, she got her cue so she sauntered into the room as if she was the most important and most beautiful thing in the world. The doctor gently took the nurse by the arm and wispered in her ear that she needed to stay proffesional and that she would be watched. Then she snatched her arm away from his hand then went on with introducing herself to the couple. Now that the nurse made a complete bumbling idiot of herself the doctor spoke up saying that he really needed her at another task but he knew who would be better suited for the position then the nurse puffed up and made some childlike noises and stomped off after her dramatic stage exit. The doctor admitted that the nurse got fired for her unruly behavior and sent to a facility that specializes in behavior modification, apparently it did not help her.

The doctor admitted that the nurse would never work for any kind of medical related job but he did have a wonderful nurse practitioner that was highly recommended and that she was on her way as they spoke. It was past due for the doctor to get going so he quickly advised Philip to keep aware of his surroundings as well as Arlene's and that he was going to have two of their men who worked the border of their community even though there had never been any situations. What the doctor was worried about was the snotty nurse that was sent away stalking the couple and possibly taking things to another level after showing up again. To what level she would raise the level of care was unknown for it was not predictable. The border patrolman would stay in the living room to be able to view most things. Arlene informed the doctor that it might be better if there were two border patrol men that could have twelve hours to do their jobs and twelve to rest up and eat then the doctor told Arlene that she had a grand idea and he would set that up immediately.

As the doctor was on his way out he made sure that there were two border patrol men set aside to leave the border of their colony and go to Philip and Arlene's home to start their new orders. The border patrol men got to the couples front door at the same time as the nurse practitioner. The men used their manners and while holding the door open they stood off to the side and softly told the nurse practitioner who they were and that they were there to assist them. After she went in, the patrolmen went in . The three of them went to Philip to make sure he knew they were there, what their orders were, and that they would follow their orders if they veered off of the set orders. Philip informed the three of them that for now the two men were off until midnight then one of them could start to work then at noon the other one could take over while the other could eat and get some food and whatever else was needed. The nurse practitioner sat in the bedroom with Arlene just talking about good memories and things that were missed from before getting into the colony but extremely grateful that they were chosen to have their lives extended then they praised God and moved on to sharing who they were personally like honest, forgiving, helpful, very upfront, and so on the two of them were having a great time and they were actually bonding the nurse practitioner questioned Arlene if she had played with boy and girl names yet and Arlene sighed then in a low tone replied no but added in a regular tone if she would be willing to kick around some names with her and Philip then the nurse lit up and cheering popped out that she would love to that it would be an honor how special did it get than to offer fun assistance to the king and queen of their community. During the elongated conversation the nurse was checking out Arlene and found out that she was dilated to three centimeters so she hollard out for Philip to get the doctor right away and not to return without the doctor.

Fortunately the doctor had just closed the front door so it should be easy to catch up with the doctor and as told the runner got the doctor rather quickly and drug him back to the bedroom at Arlene's head so the nurse could deal with whatever issue had come about. The nurse informed the doctor of her findings then he asked Arlene some basic questions and she answered them. The doctor realized that Arlene was in the begining stage of labor and there was no way to turn back now so the doctor told the nurse glove-up, were about to bring a new life into our community. Arlene had not been having true contractions but that had since changed. It was not as bad as it could get. Every time she had a contraction the doctor and nurse told Arlene to push and she did and with each contraction they were getting stronger and longer. Suddenly the doctor called out that the baby was not able to pass through the vaginal canal which led the doctor to the situation when he would have to sedate Arlene so the crowning which the nurse told the couple that it meant that the baby's head was starting to come out and by now she was as fully dialated now things were going to move along rather quickly as long as the birth was not complicated. In other words as long as the baby did not birth with the presentation of one of it's limbs or the baby could not get through the birthing canal in those situations and more the doctor would do an emergency cesarean section for the safety of mom and baby but the doctor would have to perform a spinal block. First and foremost under full sedation the doctor would have to put Arlene under deep sedation and work swiftly because the medication given to Arlene would affect the baby also.

There would be a set of duties already in line and the doctor had already had the steps in mind which was setting his tray up for use for the upcoming steps. The doctor was really witty and had never been less than semi-perfect for his job in the community. It was a blessing from God above that the doctor knew for sure that he was blessed for without being blessed he would not be able to perform otherwise. Okay, now having Arlene sedated heavily the doctor performed the cesarean section and the nurse practitioner came close to help with the baby while the doctor focused on Arlene. Soon enough both mother and child were back to normal and introduced to one another, it was rather angelic then Philip interupted politely sugesting that his daughter being so angelic that it would only be right in naming their baby Natasha-star and there it was settled because everyone in the room felt like Philip, it was perfect. While Philip had everyone's attention there he proceeded to take the baby out of of his wife's limp arm's to take Natasha-Star into his arms then her husband, Philip suddenly sauntered to the back door with the baby in his arms then the baby started to cry softly out of hunger so Philip suggested going to the loving garden to show the new child the beautiful heavens of paradise and they also wanted Arlene to join them as well as the doctor, the nurse practicioner, the new helpers that may have been called in. Once there they could find a good sitting spot then Philip would give Natasha-Yar back to Arlene so she could then breastfeed Natasha-Yar while appreciationing the second hand heavens.

Soon the paradox would open and the new smell of Natasha-Star would awaken the bewildered with the love and respect for the child filled the air as if they were calling out to every living entity to show up to welcome the new child into their den as a part of their personal family, and yes Natasha-Yar had the God given ability to understand all the mythological animals and the regular animals and they to her. They took on her protection and the animals would cry out for God and God was always there then the people would march on beside the animals. The protection was of the ultimate protection for the royal family and accessible at any time therefore With Beelzebub locked away by God he would never be a proper or improper threat to anyone or anything, that went for his millions and possibly millions more of Beelzebub's millions but they were not easy for them to hide because they were clumsy and therefore they could not stay hidden at all. The minions not only could not hide but they were in few and were very childlike, they could not function without following instructions and having them repeated many times. They were extremely unable to function by their own decisions for they had no decision making skills whatsoever. The minions would suffer the low heat because the temperature was over one hundred in hell and a simple seventy above but what would be the most likely to kill them off was their deficits because their frolicing about would help heep them warm to some degree but not quite enough. Soon when it was evident there was not enough natural warmth to keep them alive and once dead their bodies would turn to ash within three seconds. Their ashes would blow away even if indoors the ashes would find a way to get outside and move onto its preset destiny as set by God. The town's people would be able to see them as they truly were without any ability to cloak themselves so nothing could see them, the past was now moving on and the town people would then be able to see them as they really were and hopefully life could go on smoothly.

Well there was enough time for Beelzebub and his minions, now back at the heavenly garden where the royal family, the doctor, the nurse practitioner, individuals who were called in by the medical runner as well as the medical runner, and those who were not mentioned but did receive an invite on the medical situation at hand. It was to be a gathering for the safety of mom and baby. Even though the birth got a tad bit longer than expected it was pretty much a safe delivery after all. Now with everybody in the heavenly garden all finding a place to sit comfortably and enjoy the beauty of God's second hand heaven. It was so overwhelming. Finally, Philip handed Natasha–Yar to Arlene so the child could get her first meal and be satisfied then after being burped she would fall asleep for a while. With a strict observation they could find out what kind of schedule Natasha-Yar would be on so if Arlene needed to change it they could do it. Although it may take some time with a slim possibility that they would not need to change the infant's schedule, everyone would work on changing the time together if it was necessary. Arlene let the individuals in her little group that was in the heavenly garden know she was ready to get dressed and go into the streets on a horse and show the town the new member of their colony and give the baby's name. The nurse practitioner replied that the two of them should go to the walk in closet and see what would be appropriet someone could let the stable boy know how many horses to dress and whether or not to set up the buggy so the doctor that birthed the baby went to the stable to let the stable boy know what he wanted and to make it special for the queen had the baby and was extremely serious about revealing the newcomer to the rest of the colony.

At the end of the ride the stable boy who would take the lead of Arlene's horse so all could see the child in her mothers arms while the stable boy shared the baby's name by speaking loudly over and over that the new addition was a girl named Natasha-Star everyone would gather around them and grow even closer than they would want to coddle the baby but Arlene spoke up saying that soon she was going to have a dinner gathering with all the kinds of foods that they could wish for and they would get to hold Natasha-Star each and everyone of them. The day and time would arrive as an invitation at their doors in time for proper preparation. As for the nurse practitioner and Arlene, they had finally found what they considered the perfect gown and even went to find Philip's attire after getting Arlene dressed then when the two of the ladies left the walk in closet with the kings clothing in the nurses hands, she handed them to Philip when they got right up to Philip then notified him that he was to go and get dressed then get himself back and he was on a timer. He had three minutes to get the transition done and be back to his current position. Philip took his clothing from the nurse and hurriedly went to the walk in closet to change clothes and he switched clothes like wild fire then he ran back to his place at Arlene's side then the nurse blurted out to Philip that they were about to send out a search party to find him for he was right at post at the three minute mark, then she laughed and he chuckled. Philip told the nurse practioner she was just joking. Now it was time for the baby nurse to transform Natasha-Star from just a regular baby to a royal baby. The baby had to get her diaper changed and get cleaned up then go back to her mother for a good feeding. After all of that had been done with the baby then the baby would be placed into Arlene's arms.

It was time to get to the barn to get up on the horses and buggy to do what Arlene wanted to do. The extra trained building workers were working overtime building a golden stroller and buggy they finished so as the buggy and stroller had become finished just as the crew was ready for their first time out, the stroller and buggy were quickly revealed to the couple then left in the barn until the time came to have the entire colony over for the dinner where everyone would get to handle the newborn and ask questions and get responses. Meanwhile the couple mounted their horses while the doctor and nurse practitioner got aboard a buggy sitting up front then the rest of the uncovered part of the buggy was for the rest of the regular nurses so everyone could see and give some credit to the others who had helped. Then behind that was the medical runner on his horse and the two of them were dressed up also. The royal runner went out to the route that they would be following to make sure that all was in order. The community officers were in check as to where to be to keep the royal family safe so at the end of the route the royal runner turned around and went up the chosen route to head back to the royal barn to prepare for the show ride for the baby. Along the way the royal runner found a young lady on the ground holding her leg just below the knee with the lead to her horse in the other hand. As he got closer he realized that the woman was Camillia.

The royal runner stopped and asked Camillia if he could help her in any way. She explained that her horse bucked her off then showed some sort of pain but she did not know what to do. The royal runner dismounted his horse and said he would check her horse then he found out what was wrong with the horse. The horse partially lost a shoe and with that he felt quite a bit of pain. What the royal runner needed to do was to get that shoe the rest of the way off then they could walk him the rest of the way back to the royal barn and get him reshoed but first he had to get Camillia onto his horse and he would walk both horses into the royal barn which would only take a few minutes. The royal runner told Camillia to hold onto her horse's lead and to not let go. Then he picked up the girl and put her atop his horse then he took the hoof that was partially unhoofed and got the hoof the rest of the way off. It was now time to walk the horses to the barn of the royal ones where they could get the horse re-shooed.

On the way the royal runner conversed with the girl and learned that her name was Camillia and she was single then the royal runner asked if it was possible for him to invite her to dinner and if she would show up then Camillia said yes definitely. She would love to join in then he replied that he was honored then Camillia broke down and revealed that she had her eyes on him for quite some time but was afraid of being rejected so she did not know how to approach him. Camillia came forward and asked the royal runner if they could work on becoming boyfriend and girlfriend then the royal runner replied that her feelings were just the same as his. The royal runner got bold and asked Camillia if she would be his girl and she replied yes certainly. The royal runner admitted that he had already gotten rings in hopes that he could give her an engagement ring and he could wear a promise ring. She said that she was ready to marry him right away but they should take things a little slow. The royal runner took the rings out of his pocket and put the ones for her on her finger and let her put the one for him on his finger. Things were at a stopping point because they had to respect the king and queen's viewing of the baby but there would be a time for them to share their news with the public in due time and the royal runner figured that nobody would have seen that coming and that made things even more wonderful. Now they were back at the royal barn and everyone noticed that the royal runner was walking and holding the leads of both horses then the doctor questioned the royal runner why he was walking both horses with a young woman on his horse. The royal runner explained that he found the young woman on the ground holding her leg just below her knee and the leed of her horse after his shoe became particially off then he bucked her off which may have broken her leg. The doctor took a look at Camellias leg and informed her that she was lucky the bone did not seem to be broken but he would like to do an x-ray to be sure but he had never been wrong before.

The doctor told Camillia that things appeared normal and she was not in pain any more so he would let her enjoy the festivities and right after they would immediately get to the hospital and take care of her leg. Arlene watched the royal runner and Camillia for a short bit and came to the conclusion that they would make a wonderful couple so Arlene told Philip, Camellia, and the royal runner to come to dinner that evening so even they agreed then they said they would make it so then Arlene sent Philip to let the kitchen staff know they were to prepare a feast for they were to entertain company with a sensitive topic. While Philip was absent the doctor presented himself in a way to focus himself on the lovely forbiden child. The doctor looked deep into his transportable microscopic scope and found out the child was cleared of any illnesses so God appeared iridescently with tears of joy as God continued to surround the colony and he made sure all sicknesses were strewed as God flourished the Camillia child with rose petals along the path they would be traveling and the petals were a blessing from God as they fell from the heavens and settled into a nestled space where God paved the way with rose petals as it led to their destination where they were needed for the viewing of the newborn Natasha-star child. Now it was time for the viewing of the baby so the stable doors were pushed open by the stable boy and everyone started to step out in proper order and kept their pace at a comfortable pace for the community and those who were walking who were in the parade.

The parade went well everyone kept their voices down when they realized the baby was asleep Arlene and Philip were thankful because as long as she was asleep all would be well for as soon as she would wake she would start to cry for mama milk and a diaper change and they would rather do all of that in the privacy of their home. Now it was time to turn around and let the people on the other side of the road get to see Natasha-Star and head to their stable to get the horses comfortable by undressessing them. Each horse was undressed and getting ready to be in their stalls for a short bit to get cleaned up then ready for being out in the fields to roam for a shorter bit then to be transferred to the hospital so the girl that was tossed off her horse and the royal runner could get back to the royal homestead. The doctor and the girl that was bucked off her horse were left at the hospital and someone followed to undress the horses and tie them up at the pole right outside the hospitals front door so when they were done they would see their horses as soon as they opened the huge door then the individual that was chosen to follow and take care of the couple went back to the royal barn and now that everyone was settled down and there was only one thing left to do which was to find the correct helpers to get the rest of the nails on the horses shoe off and get a new shoe fitted and put on the horses hoof then walk him around a bit then got on him and took a small ride in the fenced in area. In both situations the horse proved to be good to go.

Well the horse was fixed so now it was time to check on Camillia and the doctor, the x-ray was done and the doctor took the x-ray to the room that Camillia was in and proceeded to put the picture on the table light so Camillia could see the picture and see what the doctor was going to be talking about. The doctor explained that the bones were not broken but even worse it was all soft tissue damage. It would take a while to heal, in fact, it would have been better if she had broken the bone. The doctor would be checking up on Camillial when he could and it would most likely be at random then Camillia replied softly that she would be off her leg and that the royal runner would be at her home until things were back to normal if the royal couple would grant their wish. The doctor said he would speak with the royal couple immediately so he left the room and out of the hospital straight to the castle where the royal couple should be. If not the royal couple would have to be found. However, that would not be addressed until it happened because it may not be something to happen. When the doctor got to the castle and pulled the chain that when pulled, rang a hearty bell and a worker would answer the door and help the visitor to have any wishes addressed.

The doctor told the staff person that it was urgent that he speak to the royal couple. The man took the doctor through the castle to where the royal couple was and announced the doctor.

The couple acknowleged the doctor and welcomed him so the doctor spoke to the couple and let them know that Camillia would have to be on bedrest for quite some time and that their stable boy offered to take care of her. In fact they held a secret and it was that they were a couple and they were already wearing rings but they chose to not tell a soul until things became quiet. They wanted the showing of the baby to have her time because that was more important and she was waiting for the right time then the doctor respectfully asked if the royal couple would be able to get by with a substitute until their stable boy could return. The royal couple spoke about the royal runner and Camillia being a couple and that they kept it confidential. Arlene nudged Philip because she decided that they needed to allow the royal runner to be paid for his time out because he was doing some work and the royal couple would go give the new young couple the good news the doctor needed to get back to the hospital so the royal couple followed the doctor out and rode with the doctor. Once at the hospital everyone left their horses with the stable boy and he took special care of the royal horses and Arlene left the baby with the nursery nurse so now at the hospital room they announced themselves as they walked into the room. Camillia was happy to see the royal couple then the royal runner started to try to politely request some time off. Philip gently took the royal runner by the arm and started to talk and the first thing he said was that he wanted, and right then Philip interrupted and ordered for everyone to stay silent until he was finished with what he had to say. He would let them know that he was done then they were free to speak.

Now with it being Philip's time he explained that he knew that Camillia sustained a terrible injury and needed total care for quite some time. He turned to his royal king and told him that he and his wife Arlene had not been able to discuss the situation but looking back at their decision it would be the same outcome. Philip turned to Camillia and told her that he, the royal runner, could take as much time off that Camillia needed. Philip added that he would be getting paid as if he was working and after the situation was cleared he would be given something special along with Camillia. With the talk as it was being wrapped up the doctor peeked his head into the room saying that the nurses were getting her discharge papers ready. Once that was complete they could leave. The doctor had a fill in for the royal runner and that he was already there. He was a good worker but if they had any problems to contact him immediately, however, that would not happen and the doctor was sure of that. The original royal runner expressed his deepest appreciation for Philip and Arlene's decision to allow him to take as many days down to take care of Camillia and with pay then in the middle of the royal runner's words Philip interupted and said to put that behind them and start on the fun work. The nurse had finished the release papers and peeked into Camillia's room to announce her entering then she went to Camillia's bedside to explain the discharge instructions then the royal runner picked up Camillia and walked out the front door to put Camillia on her horse then he mounted his ride and off they went to go to Camillia's home.

Now at their desired destination the royal runner got off his horse so he could tie both horses to the pole right outside the barn. He could now get Camillia off her horse and get her to bed to have the nurse help her get into something relaxing. The royal runner went back to the horses to get them situated but to his surprise they were already taken care of so the royal runner went into the barn to see if he could find the person who took care of the horses and to his surprise there was a stable boy and he started to converse with the stable boy and learned that the stable boy had been working for the royal couple since before they were royalty and he planned to stay with the royal couple until death separated them in a way that no longer required his service. The royal runner explained that he needed to cut the conversation short and why. He did invite the stable boy for dinner and a chance to converse with Arlene and get a better look at the royal baby Natasha-Star. If Arlene was up to it, possibly holding the new addition. The stable boy thanked the royal runner for the invite to dinner and said he would be there and for Philip to get back to Arlene's side so the royal runner said thanks and rushed off to get to Arlene's side to tell her about the invitation.

When the royal runner confessed to Camillia the conversation between the stable boy and himself Camillia was good with it. Camillia told the royal runner to make sure that he set everyone involved with making the necessary adjustments, the royal runner replied of course then went on to take care of the issues at hand. When done the royal runner would get back to Camillia and while he was out the nurse would be helping Camillia change clothes from extremely fancy and stiff to something more relaxed such as a one layered yet comfortable and able to be slept in night wear but appropriate to be worn in mixed company. After redressing Camillia, the nurse helped Camillia back into her bed.The royal runner arrived at Camillia's bedside. Within seconds of the nurse helping her get back into her bed Philip returned.. Everything was dealt with and caught up with so it was time for all involved to take a break for a short time then it would be dinner time. Camillia would be eating in bed but the royal runner would be close by. Relaxation period was over and it was time to serve the meal so the nurse made sure Camillia was sitting properly to be able to eat without spilling her food all over herself. Everyone else sat at the dining room table except the royal runner. He sat at the bar on a barstool to be within eyesight of Camillia and so she could see him also. Everyone had a plate of food and other parts of the meal to come.

An hour later the meal was finished and the kitchen staff was cleaning the kitchen and when done they would go home and prepare for the next day. The nurse turned into a room provided by Camillia to have hers for as long as she was needed. The royal runner had another room that Camillia told him to settle into while he was there. The royal runner checked on Camillia one last time and tucked her in bed, while he told her he loved her then she told him she loved him. He insisted that she call for him if she needed him and he would be right there ahead of everyone. Then they said goodnight to one another and the royal runner went to his room and got into the bed and everyone was finely sound asleep, their bodies working hard to replenish for the next day with whatever should be brought to them. Now that it was early in the next day the regular animals gathered to welcome the royal runner and Camillia to a new day. The mythological animals gathered around Camillia's home to help the royal runner and Camillia wake up slowly and comfortably. The centaur opened the blinds over the windows then the centaur opened the windows so the royal runner and Camillia could hear the precious sounds of the various animals including the mythological ones. Soon after the the centaur opened the house the royal runner and Camillia awoke, the royal runner sped to Camillia's bedside to tell her how much he loved her and good morning. The royal runner followed his morning greeting by asking her if she needed or simply wanted anything. Camillia replied that she was fine but to invite all the regular and mythological animals inside then it would be a great day. If she could not visit her fellow friends she felt that her day would be gloomy and destined for the negative side of things.

The royal runner did just as Camillia asked and returned to her bedside. Right behind the royal runner the animals were at his heels. Camillia sat all the way up in bed so she could greet all her friends then she pulled the blankets tight so the smaller animals could climb up and the centaur helped some of the animals that could not fly, climb, jump high, or otherwise get on the bed to visit with Camillia. The nurse was still asleep and no one was going to wake her, she was not really needed and the not so obvious couple was going to have the royal runner leave Camillia's home to retreive Arlene and Philip to see if they could have the nurse go back to her regular duties. Now that the royal couple had returned to Camillias home with the royal runner they got comfortably sat down. The royal runner explained that the nurse was no help and they believed they could take care of things on their own. The royal couple decided to keep things fair they would spy on them and the nurse in a way that their own families wouldn't even know. She could entertain inside with her family and be outside with her equiptment to take care of her responsibilities of spying on them and no one would even know except her. Arlene and Philip got the serious side of themselves in check and realized that they already had one check against the nurse. The strike against the nurse was that she had not gotten up to check on Camillia or to see if the royal runner needed any assistance in taking care of Camillia.

Since the nurse was noncompliant and was being lazy instead of taking note and firing her the royal runner wanted the royal couple to see what the nurse was and was not doing because the nurse was far more important than getting let go or fired the royal couple did not question the nurses lacking sleep. Instead the royal couple questioned the nurse who was asked if she could steer herself in a more persevering way, channeling herself in her important career of taking care of humans, a career of taking care of all types of animals which did get medical care at the hospital, and Camillia had always taken care of the animals and was great with them. Now in question by asking the nurse from the royal couple as the nurse adhered to the royal couple's voices while they awakened her. The nurse was quite rude and obnoxious which was inappropriate for the current situation. What type of mind would she be in on first contact with Camillia? The doctor had been there for a short time but long enough to know what they were talking about. The doctor spoke to the nurse about not being a proper choice for the type of care needed for Camillia. She was perfect for a job at the hospital that included more sleep and filled a position that no one else could fill. It had been open for quite some time and he felt she would love the job. He knew for sure because he had seen her assist in that type of work at the hospital and she was the only one seemingly qualified to work under the specialist for the medical job he had thought of.

The doctor exposed the position to Camillia to see if she felt that she could work over the nurse, it was being a veterinarian's assistant at the hospital where she would have her own space, use of any part of the hospital, and staff that was set aside to try to express their most deepest inner feelings to her. but they both already knew that their love was a love at first sight because they both had a lifelong royal look about their faces. The look got everyone talking that there must have been something between them because the young royal couple had several things to announce such as Camillia getting the position of the hospital's veterinarian, the nurse being her assistant, the royal runner and Camillia being engaged to be married to the rest of the people at the community hall. Arlene returned to the group so Philip felt the time to make the announcements was at hand. Arlene and Philip announced the coming out of the royal child and that all adults were welcome to attend the public gathering and that all was in place for a buffet style luncheon where everyone would get a chance to hold the royal child and it would continue until everyone had their opportunity to hold Natasha-Star.

With that announcement everyone whistled and clapped as they surprisingly sprung out of their seats. Each and every individual got into a straight line to get their turn to give Arlene and Philip a big hug and kiss on the cheek and assure them that they would be there with bells and whistles. The food hall was going to be transformed into a low key coming out party hall. Philip informed the community that they needed to go home and get ready for the party and the couple would do the same then everyone would eventually return there and the party would start and continue until everyone had their time with Natasha-Star. The baby was only two days old and due to the baby's inability to control most of her muscles especially in the neck Arlene was beyond concerned because if someone in the colony forgot to support the baby's head while handing the baby off to the next person it may result in the death of the child in a worse case scenario. Philip had been keeping an eye on Arlene and he had been aware of her discomfort with the handling of her offspring so he went to her as she followed the baby around the room by being behind every person that had the baby. Philip took Arlene by the hand and started to console her by explaining that their baby would be fine. She just had the first time mothers complex. Philip told Arlene that it would be in her best interest to go over to the food line and fill her plate while he did the same. Then together they could go sit at their original places and relax, enjoy one another and their guests, eat just a few bites of the food, and share the people's admiration of their baby besides the nurse was there to handle things.

Arlene finally got relaxed which made Philip feel less worried about his wife and she became more talkative and joking with the people at their table that made her laugh, she was back to her normal self and that made Philip quickly transform back into his normal self. There was one more gathering Arlene wanted to hold and that was with her. Philip and the nurse have over the fifty-five children that she had bonded with while in the hospital. The children were not seen because they had a lot of physical adjustments and psychological damage to fix that Beelzebub had twisted and instilled into those children; however, they were doing great and very close to being ready to go out and mix in with the other children and all of the adults. Arlene leaned into Philip and softly whispered into his ear that they needed to get word out to all those children that they were invited to their home to spend some time with them and Natasha-star. While there Arlene would help them to hold the baby and they would eat dinner with them which would allow them all more time together. Philip whispered back that he would get the royal runner to reach out to all the children and make sure they all got a written invitation to be at their home that evening right at four p.m. sharp and that pleased Arlene then when Philip was finished speaking, Arlene thanked her husband and gave him an innocent kiss on the cheek then they both went back to conversing with the others at their table.

Several hours later people started to trickle off to go back to their own homes so when the royal couple were the only people left they went home to prepare for the gathering with the children who were left at home during the adult gathering, now it was quickly approaching the time for the children's gathering and because the royal couple only lightly snacked at the adults gathering they would be able to lightly snack at the children's gathering. It was now four in the afternoon and the children were all starting to arrive one right after the other until finally all fifty five children were there and ready to spend time with Arlene, Philip, and Natasha Star. All the children found a spot to sit comfortably in preparation to hold the new baby Natasha Star where they could love on her and welcome her into the world. The nurse was there to take Natasha Star from Arlene to give to the first visiting child, then the next child and so forth and so on until each child had a chance to hold her. Each child was overcome with immense amounts of excitement as they held the child that was no bigger than their toy doll. Each child spoke to Natasha Star as if they were her Big Brother or Big Sister promising to take care of her and protect her from anything that should be upsetting or scary to her. Right as the last child was handing Natasha star to the nurse the earth started to quake. It was strong and made their houses shake, making things on the walls swing, making lights go off and on which in turn caused the children to clutch to one another in a large circle as if there was some sort of monster in their present. Natasha Star started to cry then an intense shocking bright ray of light from Natasha Star's eyes covered the entire home. Suddenly, the motion of the home ceased to shake violently and the things on the walls Stopped moving about. The lights stayed on Instead of eerily flickering.

The children looked around at one another with fearful expressions on their faces as each one to be silently asking the others what just happened. Right at that moment Arlene spoke up with a soft voice assuring the children that everything would be okay. However, Arlene noticed at that point Natasha-Star was just a day old when the original incident occurred. It went on as an awkward feeling Becoming uncomfortably overwhelming within her own body. That was somewhat familiar then within seconds everything around her turned to black as though she was blind, nothing was heard on the outside as though she was deaf, her nose and her mouth refused to work and her sense of touch was all numb. With this apparent isolation of the five senses it seemed Arlene became aware of a vision in her mind of Beelzebub, he was holding his pitchfork towards her as it released a soft cloud of white lightning like a streak of energy being released into her infant solar plexus. It gave her a warm feeling that tingled at the entrance site of her solar plexus and grew weaker as it spread over the rest of her body. He spoke to her as if he were reciting a poem while he was filling her entire newborn body with the energy like a beam of charged light. It felt rather comfortable. Arlene had been trying to hear what that ghastly beast was saying to her but it remained inaudible. That back flash was when she was just a wee little thing suddenly the vision flashed forward to when she was a toddler. Arlene averaged her age to be we will say about four years in age and in bed to take her daily nap.

Beelzebub was caressing her head and speaking poetically in this vision also. All Arlene was trying to hear was the gospel it was transmitting very broken up but it remained in-Audible. suddenly it went from a vision of her being a weird abstract thing to her being a human toddler. She did not appear to be afraid of Beelzebub, she went straight to him when he appeared to her in her room at night when everybody was asleep. Not all of the words were audible but here and there a word may have been understood. It seemed that nasty Beelzebub was trying to take her in to be something to him, he was trying to earn her trust so she could perform some sort of task for him. So much was left unknown that It was still impossible for Beelzebub to get Arlene to do as he wished. The children were tugging on Arlene's dress to get her attention because they felt that she might have been in another world in her mind and they didn't understand what she was going through. At that moment based on her frightened facial expressions it appeared to them that Arlene was somewhere where Beelzebub could once again influence her but that would be dealt with in time for the children did plan on talking to Jesus as soon as they could make sure the house was a safe place then they could summon Jesus thru prayer since none of the children had their special feathers with them and it would take time that they did not want to risk taking to go to their homes to get their feathers and return to Arlene's home.

After searching the house for unwanted guests and peeking outside all the windows it all checked out to be safe, there were no signs of danger. The children all took one another's hands as they knelt down to pray for everything they could possibly think of regarding the current situation. Once finished the children let their hands go loose from one anothers then they stood up. No sooner than when the children stood up Jesus appeared and informed them that he already knew of the situation involving Arlene and he was going to address it soon but for now she needed to be on her own for learning and growth purposes. Jesus enlightened them that Arlene was just fine, that she needed to experience what she was and that type of event would happen many times over. It was just what needed to happen to release Arlene from the claws of Beelzebub forever. Even though he was locked away where he could not reach anyone, or so that was how it was supposed to be because the children did not see it as being safe for Arlene. At that point Beelzebub Realized that he had no hold on Arlene and could not get her to succumb to his liking and therefore eventually would be back to being independent of herself.